Up in Sister Bay

To Hayward
and
Court Oreilles

Upper Arm

Up Holly Bay

Loon Lodge

Hauger's Landing

Low Holly Bay

Swede's Place

Andy's Tavern

Buhl Farm

Garbutts Island

Moonrise

West Doktor's

To Billy Sashabaw's Lake

Road to Hayward

Narrows

Old Logging Trail

Knuteson Creek

Rosenfelder's Farm

Lower Arm

Sister Bay

Soo Line Railroad

Lake
Big Chetac

Town
of
Sister Bay

Up in Sister Bay

CHARLES FERRY

Drawings by Ted Lewin

Houghton Mifflin Company Boston 1975

Library of Congress Cataloging in Publication Data

Ferry, Charles, 1927–
  Up in Sister Bay.

  SUMMARY: Relates the dreams, frustrations, and
challenges of three teenage friends growing up in
rural Wisconsin during the 1930's.
  [1. Farm life—Wisconsin—Fiction] I. Lewin, Ted.
II. Title.
PZ7.F42Up   [Fic]   75-15799
ISBN 0-395-21409-2

v 10 9 8 7 6 5 4 3 2 1

To Ruth

Up in Sister Bay

1

Coming in off Big Chetac the steeple of Holy Childhood came into view first and then the Indian mission set back in the trees behind it. The Swede cut the motor and let the *Ruby Allen* drift into the bay.

"It's the breakin' loose that's hard, Robbie," he said to the boy who sat up in the bow of the boat. "The cemetery will help."

Robbie VanEpp looked in toward the town. It was dusk. A thin haze hung over the bluffs. Lights were coming on in the houses. At the foot of Hill Street the last rays of the sun glittered off the tannery water tower, which was still streaked from the smoke of the fire.

"Should I say a prayer, Swede?" he said.

"That'd be nice, Robbie," the Swede said. "Yes, Alvia would like that."

"An 'Our Father'?"

"Oh-hh, I don't know, Robbie. Why don't you just make one up. Made-up prayers are always best."

The Swede took an oar and maneuvered the *Ruby Allen* alongside the pier that ran out from Silurian Park. Robbie climbed out and held the boat steady. The Swede handed up the basket of wildflowers that Livvie Buhl had gathered during the day.

"What're we goin' to do about Charlie, Swede?" Robbie said.

"What's there to do, Robbie?" the Swede replied. "The law's the law."

"Well, shoot, Swede, we can't just let him rot up in that jail!"

"You needn't get testy, Robbie. You ain't the first person to have somebody die on you."

"I'm sorry, Swede," Robbie apologized, "but you know Charlie didn't set that fire."

"I know nothin' of the kind, Robbie. I think Charlie didn't do it, but thinkin' it and knowin' it are two different things. People with Charlie's affliction do strange things sometimes, Robbie. It's hard to accept, but it's a fact."

The water lapped gently at the pilings of the pier. Across the bay a blue heron swooped low over the headlands, then soared up over the bluffs.

"Go on and pay your respects, Robbie," the Swede

2

said, "then hightail it home. Your ma'll be worried sick."

He pulled his straw hat down over his sunburned face and wound the starter-cord on the Evinrude.

"Is Jim back from Flambeau State Forest yet?" he asked.

"Tonight, maybe," Robbie replied, "or first thing in the mornin'. They were goin' to cut an extra stand of timber if the weather was good."

"The two of you plannin' to be up at Livvie's tomorrow?"

"I guess so," Robbie said.

"We-ll — " the Swede said, pursing his lips, "I'll run up to the courthouse and talk to Stanfill P. Stanfill. Meantime why don't you stop by Arbuckle's and pick up the gossip, okay?"

Robbie nodded. "Okay, Swede," he said.

The Swede pushed the *Ruby Allen* clear of the pier.

"It won't be easy, Robbie," he called back. "With Alvia gone the Herr Doktor'll be crackin' the whip in this town."

The sound of the outboard broke the stillness. Robbie watched the *Ruby Allen* cross the bay and veer around the headlands. He waved to the Swede and the Swede waved back, and then the boat went out of sight up the lake, the drone of the motor fading in the distance.

Robbie started up the pier. The glow of kerosene lamps came from the houses. He liked the way the town looked in the twilight. A town's character, he had learned from his grandfather, showed in the way people tended their yards and looked after their houses. When a town lost its spirit, the paint blistered and peeled and the apples rotted on the ground. Sister Bay was special. Honeysuckle grew on the chimneys, and three times a day the bells of Holy Childhood rang the Angelus.

Robbie cut through Silurian Park toward the cemetery. Down along the bay, lights were still burning at the tannery, but Main Street appeared deserted, except for a few pickups in front of Arbuckle's general store. The store didn't look right, Robbie thought, without Charlie out front hawking his worms and waving at the cars.

The cemetery was in the bluffs overlooking the bay. A little iron fence enclosed the Ivors' plot. The gate squeaked as Robbie opened it and a cool wind rustled in the trees. He took the wildflowers from the basket and arranged them atop the mound of wreaths that covered Alvia's grave. They were all down there now, he thought, the Senator and his wife, Junior and his young bride — and now Alvia, the last of the line. All that money and position, and what had it got them?

He turned and walked to the edge of the bluff. A mist was rolling in over the headlands. Across the bay the lights of the town seemed very remote. He thought of that last night with Alvia, at Billy Sashabaw's lake, Alvia crazy drunk and a wildness in her eyes, screaming at the moon in Indian-talk. And then he thought of Charlie Barrow sitting up in the county jail, frightened and confused. A great anxiety came over him. Trouble, everybody said, came in threes. Where would it strike next?

The moon was up high by the time Robbie left the cemetery and started back to town, down the Soo Line tracks to the depot and then through Silurian Park to the Indian mission. The mission was dark. Robbie scooped up a handful of pebbles and tossed them up at Jim's window. A light came on, and Robbie breathed a great sigh of relief. He would talk things over with his friend. Jim would help him straighten things out.

"Holy cow!" Jim whispered as Robbie tiptoed upstairs. "What's been goin' on anyway?"

"Shoot, I don't know, Jim," Robbie said. "The whole town's comin' apart."

Jim closed the door and turned the kerosene lamp down low. The two of them sat Indian-fashion on Jim's bed and talked in hushed tones.

"Did Sister Joan Therese tell you what's happened?" Robbie asked.

"Most of it," Jim nodded. "When did the tannery catch fire?"

"The day after you left for the Flambeau. Charlie was the only one in the building. Somebody spotted him runnin' up the street with a gas can in his hand and called the deputy."

"But what's the connection, Robbie?" Jim said. "I mean everybody talks like the fire had somethin' to do with Alvia's dyin'."

"There is no connection, Jim," Robbie said. "The Herr Doktor's been tellin' everybody Alvia had a stroke when she found out about the fire, but Mrs. Armitage says it was heart failure.''

"What's that, anyway?"

"I don't know. I guess your heart just quits. Mrs. Armitage says she was awful drunk.''

"Did you see her 'fore she died?''

"Yeah. The night of the fire. We went to Billy Sashabaw's lake. She was in pretty bad shape then too.''

Jim leaned back against the wall and let out a little whistle.

"Well," he said, "it looks like curtains for Loon Lodge without Charlie.''

"It's our fault, Jim," Robbie said. "If it hadn't been for Loon Lodge, he never would've taken that job. He was savin' up his pay for the filing fee on the homestead.''

"How's Livvie takin' it?'' Jim asked.

"Better'n I am," Robbie replied.

"I know," Jim said. "Sister Joan Therese said you weren't at the funeral.''

"Shoot, it was all a lot of bull, Jim," Robbie said. "Everybody was there just to show off, and the Herr Doktor strutted around like he owned the town and everybody in it.''

"He probably does now," Jim said. "Sister Joan Therese says he'll get the whole shebang — Moonrise, the tannery, everything.''

Robbie shook his head in bewilderment.

"You've got to stick with me, Jim," he said. "I feel

6

like I'm flyin' apart inside. Sometimes I feel like throwin' myself off the bluffs."

Jim made a fist and punched Robbie lightly on the arm.

"Don't worry, Robbie," he said, "I'll stick with you."

And then he got to his feet and pulled a wad of bills from his pocket.

"For our Loon Lodge account," he said, handing the money to Robbie. "It's the six bucks I made up in the Flambeau. That cheer you up?"

Robbie grinned. "Yeah," he said, "a little."

"C'mon," Jim said, "you'd better shake a leg home 'fore Sister Joan Therese comes stormin' up here."

As Robbie came out of Silurian Park, a lamp was burning in the bay window of the house with the wide porch at the end of Arcadian Avenue. He tiptoed up the back stairway so as not to wake his mother and undressed in the dark. The sound of a bell echoed from up the lake. It was the *Arthur T.,* the tannery launch, with an old schooner bell mounted on the bow. Schooner bells were like train whistles, Robbie thought as he slipped into bed. When you heard them at night you slept better knowing somebody was out there looking after things . . .

Far up the lake, Livvie Buhl heard the *Arthur T.* too, as she and the Swede started down the path leading through the woods to Buhl Farm. She had waited for the *Ruby Allen,* and now the Swede was seeing her safely home.

"It's as if he's slippin' away from us, Swede," Livvie

7

was saying. "He talks about death a lot and walks in the woods at night."

"It's just the funeral, Livvie," the Swede said, "and Charlie's trouble. It'll pass."

"I don't know, Swede," Livvie said, wistfully. "It started even before that. It was Alvia, I think. It wasn't right for a grown woman to be that friendly with a boy Robbie's age."

"You're imagining things, Livvie," the Swede said. "Just give him time, that's all."

And he tried to make Livvie understand what Robbie was going through. It was a difficult time, he said. You weren't a boy really and not a man either, but somewhere in between, maneuvering to bust out. At first you felt yourself bursting with the joy of things. You thought you would go on forever, that none of it applied to you, death or pain or bad luck. And so you took risks and acted crazy at times. You held your breath and dared your heart to stop. You made big plans, for you knew you could run with the best of them. And then somebody close to you died, and you worried and brooded and wondered whether life would betray you before you got a fair chance at it.

" 'Tain't easy, Livvie," the Swede said. "Seventeen's a difficult age for a boy."

Later, in her bedroom in the big old farmhouse across the lake from Moonrise, Livvie took her secret journal from under the mattress and, with the wick of the lamp turned low, made an entry in it.

8

Robbie is afraid he'll die before he figures things out. He says once you figure things out you're free as a blue heron soaring on the north wind, which is the clean wind, the pure wind, the wind of the silver-blue light.

Robbie is so sweet! When the time comes I will comfort him with my loins, as in the Bible, and everything will be all right.

Oh, I wish the world would hurry up!

2

They had been friends for so very, very long, and now they felt it all coming apart. It was as if they were approaching some great milestone that would change their lives forever, for even in Sister Bay, they were discovering, life and good fortune were given and were taken away, without reason, without warning.

In the closeness of their relationship they had become like parts of a whole. Livvie was the wisest, Robbie the most imaginative, Jim the most resourceful. Each was strong where the other was weak, but Charlie, they all agreed, was the strongest of all, for he had so much to overcome simply to stay in place.

Charlie had once fished Robbie from the bay half-drowned. Robbie had no memory of it, but he remembered the time he had fallen from the ranger's tower and broken his ankle, and Charlie had carried him on his back four miles to Hauger's Landing.

"Don't w-w-worry, Robbie," he kept saying, "I'll g-g-get you home okay."

Charlie had been nine years old then and Robbie five, but even then there were signs of the strange affliction that would confuse Charlie's mind and eat away his muscles.

"But can't they send him to a hospital or somethin'," Robbie had asked Charlie's sister Violet, who ran the Dew Drop Inn, "and fix him up?"

"There's nothin' they can do, Robbie," Violet said. "Poor Charlie!"

And so Charlie had made a place for himself and his worms in front of Arbuckle's, an oddity to the rest of the town but a very special person to Robbie and Jim and Livvie.

"The Charlie Barrows of the world are very precious," Sister Joan Therese had told them. "They were put here to test us."

In the early years, Jim had come down from the reservation only in the summer when his father did odd jobs around the lake, and the two of them lived in a little shed behind Hauger's. Robbie's earliest memory of Jim was of a dark, brooding boy who could whittle a piece of wood into wondrous objects.

"Will you teach me how?" Robbie had asked.

"It takes patience," Jim had said. "Indians have more patience than white folks."

"How come?"

"On account of they're Indians."

Every summer Jim's arrival would be an event for Robbie and Livvie, and there would be warm, lazy months fishing the Low Holly and roaming the woods and helping with the Guernseys up at Buhl Farm.

The farm was a place of unexpected delights. Below the landing there was a shallow inlet thick with reeds and water lilies and speckled frogs that leaped from pad to pad. Raspberries grew wild along the hedgerow, and black bears came down from the hills at night to forage in the yard.

"Let's have our own farm when we grow up," Robbie had suggested one summer.

"Livvie and Charlie too?"

"Sure, all of us," Robbie said. "That way we could stick together forever."

Jim had pricked their fingers with his knife, and they had sealed the covenant in blood.

"Up Holly Bay would be b-b-best," Charlie had advised them, and suggested a name. "Loon Lodge. There's l-l-loons everywhere up there."

They had gone down to town hall and pored over the plats. It was state land, the man had told them. You got the land for free, providing you worked it and improved it.

12

"We'll keep it a secret," Robbie had said. "Somebody else might get the same idea."

And then one cold winter night Robbie had been wakened by noises outside. He slipped out of bed and went to the window. Mr. Buhl's pickup was pulled up in the driveway, and a little crowd was standing in the snow in the glow of the headlights: Robbie's mother and father, Livvie and Mr. Buhl, Mr. and Mrs. Houtekier from next door, and Jim, wearing oversized galoshes and all bundled up in blankets.

"There's been some trouble, Madelyn," Mr. Buhl was saying to Robbie's mother. "Would you mind puttin' Jim up till we can make arrangements?"

"Of course, Henry," Madelyn VanEpp said. "Jim, you and Livvie run on up to Robbie's room."

"He'll be needin' some clothes too, Madelyn," Mr. Buhl had said. "Everything got burned. They found him wanderin' in the snow without a stitch."

"Lands!" Mrs. Houtekier had exclaimed. "Miracle the boy got out alive!"

Jim and Livvie had spent the rest of the night at Robbie's. For a while Jim just sat quietly on the edge of one of the spare beds and stared at the wall. Then he crawled under the covers and started crying. Livvie had crawled in with him and held him tight.

"Don't cry, Jim boy," she had whispered, rocking Jim's head. "We'll look after you."

The government man had wanted to send Jim to an Indian orphanage out in Pennsylvania, but Sister Joan Therese wouldn't hear of it.

"They're not going to shut that boy up in an institution and kill his spirit!" she had declared.

She had gone up to see Stanfill P. Stanfill, the district attorney, ready to do battle. In the end, they had worked out a compromise. Jim would live at the mission and attend Holy Childhood until he graduated from eighth grade, but then he would have to board at the Federal high school up on the reservation.

"The boy's got to be with his people, Sister," the government man had argued.

"Nonsense!" Sister Joan Therese had protested. "We're his people now."

"But I'm trying to be fair about it, Sister. You'll still have him at the mission summers and for Christmas and Thanksgiving vacations."

"And Easter?"

"All right," the government man had sighed wearily. "Easter too."

Finally, Sister Joan Therese had agreed.

"I suppose half a loaf is better than none," she had said, and as the years flew by, she fussed over Jim as if he were her own son.

The abrupt change in Jim's circumstances left them all with a deep concern over the uncertainty of things. Loon Lodge began to take on a new urgency in their minds. By some great stroke of fortune, they were convinced, they had been born into the best of all possible worlds. Loon

14

Lodge would preserve that world and make it safe forever.

And so over the years they had planned and prepared. But now, with dark clouds gathering over distant continents, the guarantees of youth were running out. They were being put to the test, and they wondered if things would ever be the same again.

3

Robbie was awake at dawn. It was Friday. There would be his pumpkins to tend to and errands to run for Mr. Houtekier next door and the Loon Lodge sign to shellac. Mrs. Armitage had asked him to clean out the stables today — then he remembered Alvia was dead, and that there would be no more Friday afternoons at Moonrise. It was funny how it was when somebody died, he thought. Time seemed to stand still, and there was a hollowed-out feeling to everything.

He looked out the window toward the Houtekiers'. A light was still burning downstairs. Mrs. Houtekier was probably worse, he thought; there had been screams in the night. He would take her some chrysanthemums. Flowers might help ease the pain. And he would tie up

16

her clematis vines against the strong autumn winds. Wilma Houtekier's clematis arbor was the envy of the town. Everybody had said the vines wouldn't survive the first winter, but she had pulled them through and nursed them along till now they were strong and hardy with lovely blooms. She had the touch, Robbie thought. Plants always knew.

"Your pumpkins are huge this year, Son," Madelyn VanEpp said from the kitchen window when Robbie came down to breakfast.

"It was the manure that did it," Robbie said, "and the alfalfa I plowed under."

"Are you going to enter them in the harvest festival?"

Robbie shook his head. "Mr. Rosenfelder's will win," he said. "His pumpkins always win."

"You're not afraid of losing, are you?" his mother asked.

Robbie grinned sheepishly. "Yeah," he said, "I guess I am."

He slumped into a chair and took a sip from the mug of hot cocoa that was waiting for him.

"You were late last night," Madelyn VanEpp said.

"I went to the cemetery," Robbie said. "Livvie picked some wildflowers."

Madelyn VanEpp took a little envelope from the pocket of her apron.

"Sally Armitage was worried about you," she said. She handed the envelope to Robbie. "She gave me this. It's the money Alvia owed you."

"I'm sorry, Mom," Robbie said, stuffing the envelope into his back pocket, "but I just couldn't."

Madelyn VanEpp sighed. "It's all right, Robbie," she said. "I suppose Alvia would have preferred the wildflowers. I just wish you'd let me know about these things."

She brought Robbie's breakfast to the table, French toast with maple syrup and bacon, and then got a little pile of mail from the sideboard.

"Your Aunt Lib's coming up next weekend," she said.

Robbie looked up from his plate and frowned.

"How come?" he said. "Dad didn't get that job, did he?"

"No," his mother replied. She poured herself a cup of coffee from the stove and took it to the table. "She just wants to see Wilma before — well, before she gets any worse.

Robbie let out a sigh of relief.

"Holy cow," he grinned, "you had me worried for a minute."

Madelyn VanEpp sipped her coffee and studied her son. Perhaps if he had had a brother or a sister, she thought. His attachments were too strong for his own good, and one day he would be hurt. He attached himself to plants and animals, people and places, and once formed, the attachment was lasting. She had never known him to break a friendship.

"Does it mean that much to you, Son," she said, "staying in Sister Bay?"

Robbie smeared a piece of French toast with butter.

"It's my town, Mom," he said.

"Yes, I suppose it is," his mother said. "I just thought that with Alvia dying and Charlie's trouble you might feel differently. Well — you're safe for a while, till you finish high school anyway, but your father's determined."

Robbie finished his breakfast and watched his mother puttering about the kitchen. There was a gentleness in her, he thought, that was lacking in his father. He loved his father but never felt at ease with him. His father carped at him and embarrased him in front of his friends. Every month when his father's government check came he would come home mean drunk from Hugo's, and Robbie would hear him downstairs hollering and saying cruel things to his mother. At those times he hated his father and wished him dead, and afterward he would feel guilty about it.

"Mom?" Robbie said. "If Dad gets that job down in Chicago why couldn't I stay here in Sister Bay? I could probably get on at the tannery or somethin'."

"Oh, Robbie, that's ridiculous!" his mother said. "Your father wants you to go to college. Besides, Chicago's a fine city. When we were on our honeymoon, we went dancing at the Edgewater Beach, right out on the lake. It was so lovely — "

But Robbie had a different memory of Chicago, the dirt and the tramps and the run-down flats along the el on the way out to visit Aunt Lib. You could look right in the windows of the flats, the train came so close. Sometimes

19

you would see a guy slapping his wife around, or a guy puking in the sink. There were hardly any trees, and the only flowers were what grew in little wooden boxes under windows.

It was a lousy way to live, he thought, not at all like Sister Bay, where there was a swing on the porch and a weather vane on the roof and the neighbors did the housework when somebody died. The house on Arcadian Avenue was warm in the winter and cool in the summer, and there was a pump on the sink to bring rainwater up from the cistern. There was even a grapevine and casks of sweet red wine made from the grapes. When Robbie was little, his grandfather would let him have a sip before he went to bed. He would get into his pajamas and go down to the cellar, and Gramps would pour the wine right from the cask, through a little wooden spigot that squeaked when you turned it. The wine would feel warm in your belly, and you would sleep like a log.

"Be sure and stop by the Houtekiers' before you start up to Livvie's, Son," Madelyn VanEpp said, "and see if Odie has anything that needs doing."

"Yes, ma'am," Robbie said.

"And tell Wilma I got her a mass card for Alvia but there's no one to send it to."

"You could send it to Mrs. Armitage," Robbie said. "She's stayin' over at Couderay with her nephew."

"Yes, Sally Armitage would appreciate that," Madelyn VanEpp said. "It must have been a blow to her. She practically raised Alvia."

She cleared away the dishes and got the dishpan out from under the sink. There was a snag in one of her stockings, Robbie noticed, and her heels were run-down and the paraffin she kept packed in one of her front teeth to hide the cavity had fallen out.

It was funny about parents, Robbie thought. You never imagined them as ever having been young. Maybe hard times cheated them of their youth and made them grow up early. Sometimes his mother would get very tired and look very sad and wonder out loud if things would ever get better.

Still, Sister Bay wasn't nearly as bad off as some places. Everybody was hard up, but they ate well and dressed well and looked after one another. It was the land that did it, Robbie knew. It made a difference when you had land. The land fed you and gave you possibilities.

The Swede said times were hard or not depending upon who you were. There were kids Robbie's age riding the rods, he said, and slaving for a penny an hour in the yellow-dog sweatshops. It was the cities, Robbie was convinced. The cities made things unmanageable and turned people ugly.

Besides, you couldn't grow pumpkins in a window box.

4

Robbie and Indian Jim maneuvered the birch-bark canoe through the Narrows with a practiced skill, paddling hard to avoid the pilings of the old trestle. Ahead, the upper arm of Big Chetac stretched out long and blue and beautiful.

"Hard port!" Jim called out as the canoe brushed one of the pilings.

There was always a sense of satisfaction in clearing the Narrows, Robbie thought. The Narrows was tricky. The current was swift and the channel deep, except for along the banks, where it was shallow and muddy and the willows hung so low you had to push the branches out of the way.

"She's actin' up today," Robbie said as they broke free

of the current and lurched into the choppy waters of the upper arm.

It was good out on the lake, he thought. The lake was uncomplicated, and your cares fell away. He scanned the clear blue sky for signs of the weather. A storm was brewing somewhere, probably up over the big lake and maybe an autumn blow. It would reach them in a day or two, by Monday for sure. Big Chetac could be treacherous when it stormed. He veered the canoe in toward calmer waters. They sat there for a minute catching their breath.

"Look, Jim." Robbie pointed to a flat, gray-fringed cloud scudding down over Garbutt's Island. "An autumn cloud, and it's still August."

Jim nodded. "It'll be an early autumn," he said. "It's been a dry summer, and it'll be an early autumn."

"Remember the year of the forest fires?" Robbie said. "It was so dry the leaves turned color in July."

Jim pulled his hat down against the wind. It was a Chippewa hat, black with a wide brim and a cardinal feather that stuck out from the band.

"We'll have to hunt grouse," he said, " 'fore the snow comes."

"And deer," Robbie said. "We'll send smoke signals after you get up to Court Oreilles."

"Same code as before?"

"Yeah," Robbie replied, "only let's add a couple new ones in case we decide to hunt the Flambeau or somethin'."

"Should we take Livvie?"

"Shoot," Robbie said, "Livvie's strong enough for anything now. We could take Charlie too."

"Yeah," Jim said, "if he's out of jail by then."

"Don't worry, Jim boy, he'll be out long before then."

"I've been thinkin', Robbie," Jim said. "What if it turns out Charlie really did it?"

Robbie rested his paddle across the gunwales and leaned over to scoop a drink from the lake.

"Shoot, Jim," he said, letting the cool water trickle down his chin, "Charlie'd never do anything mean."

"But there's his illness, Robbie. Maybe he had a spell and went crazy for a minute."

"Bull!" Robbie said. "Just because he's sick don't mean he's crazy like the Herr Doktor says. Otherwise why would they have hired him at the tannery in the first place?"

"Yeah," Jim said, "I guess you're right."

Robbie swung the canoe back into the wind. On the lake Robbie was the leader. In the woods Jim naturally took command, but Robbie was the leader on the lake.

"C'mon," he said, "we'll make better time close to shore."

They bore down hard on their paddles. The waves buffeted the canoe.

"Look at it blow!" Jim hollered.

With the exception of Moonrise and the Herr Doktor's place adjoining it, all of the farms and resorts were on the western shore of Big Chetac, along the narrow dirt road

24

that wound the length of the lake, then curved up toward Hayward, the county seat. Buhl Farm was midway on the upper arm, then came Andy's tavern and the Swede's Place. Above the Swede's a path led through the birch woods around Low Holly Bay to Hauger's Landing & Boatworks, where the *Arthur T.* came in.

"There's Livvie," Jim said as the rocky and thickly wooded shoreline opened on the rolling fields of Buhl Farm.

It was a small farm but pretty, the house set back in an elm grove between the pasture and a little alfalfa meadow. The barn was painted green with white trim, the only green barn on the lake. Robbie looked for Livvie and spotted her, a blur of red-checked gingham racing down the hedgerow, her long chestnut hair trailing in the wind and her voice carrying out over the water, clear as a bell.

"Halloo, Robbie! Halloo, Jim boy! Ma's waitin' lunch on you!!"

"Halloo, Livvie!" Jim called back. "I made six bucks at the Flambeau!"

It was a good feeling, Robbie thought, paddling in toward shore, the water choppy and cold, with the good smells drifting out from the farm and Livvie waving from the pier. The cemetery seemed a million years ago. It was Jim and Livvie, he knew. And the farm. Farms always made him feel good.

5

From the window next to the big black iron cookstove, Lela Buhl watched Livvie and Jim and Robbie as
they came up from the landing. She was a stout woman
who always looked cool, even with the heat of the stove,
in her starched cotton prints and with the scent of lilac
powder about her.

"They'll want to see Charlie," she said to her husband
as he came in from his chores.

Henry Buhl stomped his hightops on the horsehair mat
and took the coffeepot to the table.

"Charlie's their friend, Lela," he said. "He nursed
their cuts and bruises. We've no right to interfere."

"Folks will talk, Henry."

"Folks always talk, Lela. It's when they stop talkin' you've got to worry."

Lela Buhl returned to the window. Robbie and Jim were boosting Livvie into one of the elms to tease a squirrel. It was always the three of them, she thought, out on the lake or off in the woods or helping Charlie with his worms down at Arbuckle's. But Robbie and Jim were good boys; there was no denying that. And she and Henry were beholden. Lands, the way they had worked with that child! Egging her up the rope to the hayloft and throwing her up on old Blinky, the plow horse — *"You can do it, Livvie! You can do it!"* — and when she fell off, throwing her right back up again, the poor girl whimpering from the pain and that ugly steel brace clattering to beat the band. There would be pain, Dr. Murray had warned them; there would be much pain —

"The sow's ready for slaughter, Lela," Henry Buhl said, coming to the stove for a bowl of bean soup. "Figured I'd get around to it this afternoon."

"Then you don't think we should cancel?" Lela Buhl said. "I mean, with all the trouble?"

"It's only a potluck, Lela," Henry Buhl said. "No sense in payin' trouble more than its due."

Lela Buhl got the butter crock from the icebox and took it to the table. Henry was right, she supposed, but sometimes it was best to let things set, to let folks adjust. It wasn't just Alvia's dying and Charlie's trouble. There was Wilma Houtekier to think of. It would be a disrespect, a lot of drinking and dancing with Wilma wasting away. Poor Odie! It had been one thing after another. She would miss Wilma. There weren't many of the old-timers left, and now with defense plants springing up all over and farm families flocking to the cities —

"Henry?" she said. "Is Nate VanEpp back from Chicago yet?"

"Not that I heard," Henry Buhl replied. "Probably tootin' it up a bit, if I know Nate."

"Maybe," Lela Buhl said, "or maybe he landed that job he was after."

She stirred the bean soup and watched it bubble up. There was a comfort in cooking.

"It would break Livvie's heart, Henry," she sighed, "if Robbie was to move away. Those kids've been dreamin' of homesteadin' that land on the Up Holly for longer than they can remember."

Henry Buhl opened the copy of the *Sawyer County Record* that his wife had set next to his plate. The news from Europe was worse.

"Times are changing, Lela," he said. "A youngster ought not dream too hard."

6

The Swede didn't arrive till late afternoon. Livvie heated up the bean soup and brought a plate of bread and the butter crock to the table. It wasn't a matter of presumption, the Swede told them, it was a matter of evidence, and the plain fact was there was already more than enough evidence to convict Charlie.

"But nobody saw Charlie do it," Livvie protested.

"It don't matter, Livvie," the Swede said. "Circumstances point to it, don'tcha see? and Stan says that's what nine-tenths of the law is all about, circumstances."

Robbie let his gaze drift out the window. He knew Buhl Farm as well as his own home. Every winter he came up to shovel out the deep snows, and in spring he and Livvie helped with the planting in the sloping corn-field that bordered the pasture. And now, as they sat around the kitchen table, with the warm sunlight streaming in the window and a pot of apple butter simmering on the stove, Charlie's dilemma took on an unreal quality against the order and tranquillity of the farm.

"Then Mr. Stanfill thinks Charlie's guilty?" Jim said.

"No, Jim, as a matter of fact he don't," the Swede said. "He said if the deputy hadn't been wettin' his pants to be a big G-man Charlie probably wouldn't be in this mess. But he don't intend to let his personal judgment interfere with his duty. Once a complaint is signed and an arrest is made, it's his responsibility as district attorney to follow through on it. And he said he can't wait much longer. It wouldn't be fair to Charlie."

"Then how do things stand, Swede?" Robbie asked.

"Sort of shaky, Robbie," the Swede said. "Right now the only thing Charlie's charged with is disorderly conduct, but the way the evidence is piling up Stan will be forced to up the charge to arson."

"Poor Charlie!" Livvie said. "They'll send him to prison."

"Not likely, Livvie," the Swede said. "Stan said if it comes to that he'll ask Judge Koontz to commit him to Mendota. That is, if the Herr Doktor don't beat him to it."

"What do you mean, Swede?" Livvie said.

"Oh-hh, it seems he's been pesterin' Charlie's ma to

sign the papers, Livvie,'' the Swede said. ''And if he catches her when she's half-snockered up she might be fool enough to do it.''

''Shoot,'' Robbie said, grimacing. ''Seems Mendota's a pretty handy place to have around.''

''My ma was down there,'' Jim said, '' 'fore she died.''

''No bull?'' Robbie said.

''Uh-huh,'' Jim said. ''You ever been by there?''

''Once,'' Robbie said, ''when Gramps took me down to the state fair.''

''What's it like?''

''Spooky. It's along a lake across from the university, a lot of gloomy old brick buildings with bars on the windows.''

Livvie said, ''How long would they keep Charlie there, Swede?''

''Hard to say, Livvie,'' the Swede said. ''Stan says it's up to the judge and the doctors. I guess there are people like Charlie who've been down there most of their lives.''

They fell into silence for a moment. Then Robbie banged a fist on the table.

''Well, if that ain't the rottenest thing I ever heard!'' he said, angrily. ''Charlie's no more crazy than you or me. He got straight A's in school. Shoot, if it weren't for his handicap he could've been a chemist at the tannery or worked in the lab at the hatchery — ''

''Calm down, Robbie,'' the Swede said, ''calm down.''

''But what are we goin' to do, Swede?''

"We-ll, nothin', I'm afraid," the Swede said, "at least for a while. Stan will be out of town all next week. But he's comin' down to the Dew Drop Inn the Sunday after the potluck to see Violet. He wants to talk to you too, Robbie."

"Me?" Robbie said. "Why me?"

"He figures you might know more than you think you know, on account of your bein' so close to Alvia. Meantime, he said you could all sign a deposition testifyin' to Charlie's character."

"A deposition?" Livvie said. "What's that?"

"Oh, its kind of a sworn statement, Livvie," the Swede said. "It becomes part of the court record."

"It doesn't seem like much, does it?" Livvie said. "A statement from us against the Herr Doktor and half the town."

"No-oo, Livvie, it ain't much," the Swede said. "But Stanfill P. Stanfill's a good man. If there's a way out, he'll find it."

The Swede got up to leave.

"When will we get to see Charlie, Swede?" Robbie asked.

"Oh, in a few days probably, Robbie."

"How's he doin', Swede?" Jim said.

"He looks poorly, Jim. I don't think he understands what's happenin'."

"Poor Charlie!" Livvie sighed.

The wind clattered in the trees and whitecaps showed on the lake as Robbie and Jim and Livvie started down to the

32

landing. Livvie skipped down the hedgerow backwards, facing Robbie and Jim.

"Oh, I just love it when it's like this!" she cried, clasping her arms about herself.

"Yeah," Jim said, "we're in for a good blow."

"Isn't it funny," Livvie said, "how when you're indoors, problems seem so gloomy and complicated, but outside the wind just blows them away?"

Robbie kicked at a loose stone and sent it sailing into the brush.

"Who's goin' to write that deposition for Charlie?" he said.

"I sort of figured you would, Robbie," Jim said. "You're good with words."

"Shoot," Robbie said, "I wouldn't know where to start. You need special language for that kind of thing."

"Ask Sister Joan Therese to help you," Livvie said. "Sister Joan Therese knows everything."

Livvie held the canoe while Robbie and Jim climbed in. The wind whipped her gingham jumper up over her slender legs.

"Be careful goin' through the Narrows," she said.

"Shoot," Jim said, "We've cleared the Narrows in lots rougher weather'n this."

Livvie reached down and squeezed Robbie's hand.

"Keep faith, Robbie," she whispered, a trace of anxiety in her eyes. "If you keep faith, everything can't help but be all right."

It was growing dark when Robbie and Jim came in

around the headlands. Lights were coming on in the stores along Main Street. Above the rooftops they could see the flag coming down over the town hall.

"You still plannin' to hurl yourself off the bluffs, Robbie?" Jim said.

Robbie grinned. "Not likely, Jim," he said. "I feel lots better now."

"Good," Jim said. "You're a real pain when you're gloomy like that."

They beached the canoe and started through the park to the mission. As they parted, Jim turned to Robbie and gave him their secret handshake.

"It's swell bein' friends, isn't it, Robbie?" he said.

"Yeah, Jim," Robbie said. "I guess it's the swellest thing in the world."

Robbie turned up Arcadian Avenue. He could see his mother lighting a lamp in the parlor. There would be fried crappies for supper, he thought, with string beans from the garden and maybe cherry cobbler for dessert.

He quickened his step to get home.

7

Saturday loomed as a long, monotonous ordeal that somehow had to be endured. Robbie wished they could go up and see Charlie, but the Swede would be delivering cheese all day, and visitors weren't allowed at the jail on Sundays.

After breakfast Robbie took some chrysanthemums over to Mrs. Houtekier, and then stopped by Arbuckle's to collect Charlie's worms. The wind came up off the bay in sharp gusts.

" 'Mornin', Robbie," Shorty Arbuckle called from the counter as Robbie came into the store.

" 'Mornin', Shorty," Robbie called back.

A little bell jangled on the door, and the Grange notices

that were tacked to the stanchions flapped wildly in the wind.

"Shut the door!" hollered Herman Rosenfelder, who owned the first farm above the creamery, from his seat next to the potbellied stove, " 'fore you blow us to kingdom come!"

There were a few farm ladies in the store. Over in the dry goods section Millie Horton, the Sister Bay telephone operator, was picking through a rack of dresses.

"Was that the *Ruby Allen* I heard down on the bay Thursday night, Robbie?" Millie asked. She was a plain but good-humored girl who would no longer tell her age.

"Yeah, Millie," Robbie replied. "Why?"

Millie put her hands on her hips and stomped a foot. "That Swede!" she pouted. "He was supposed to come by for the rhubarb pie I baked him!"

"He was pretty busy, Millie," Robbie said. "He said he'll be down tonight and take you to the show up in Hayward."

Robbie pulled a straight-backed chair up to the stove. Herman Rosenfelder had his ear cocked to the radio Shorty Arbuckle kept on a little stool next to the woodbox. The news from Europe continued to be bad: "Meantime, two million German troops were reported to be massing along the Polish border . . ."

"Think there'll be a war, Mr. Rosenfelder?" Robbie asked.

"Oh, there'll be a war all right, Robbie," the old farmer replied. "No stoppin' it now."

36

"Will the United States get in it?"

"Sooner or later. Probably sooner."

"But Mr. Roosevelt says nobody wants war," Robbie said.

"Things have a way of happenin' on their own, Robbie. Besides, it'll mean jobs."

"Shoot," Robbie said, "what good's a job if you get killed?"

Shorty Arbuckle laughed from the counter.

"That ain't how it works, Robbie," he said. "The folks that get the jobs won't do the dyin', unless of course Hitler invades the United States."

Robbie tried to picture the United States being invaded, with everybody huddled around their radios listening to the news bulletins. *"German Panzers raced toward the banks of the Delaware today as American forces regrouped for a stand at Philadelphia."* Independence Hall would be in flames and the Lincoln Highway clogged with refugees. Robbie couldn't imagine it. He just couldn't imagine it.

"Didn't see you at the funeral, Robbie," Mr. Rosenfelder said, turning off the radio.

"I wasn't up to it," Robbie said.

"Didn't look right, Robbie, you bein' an employee and all."

"Shoot, it wasn't as if I was a regular employee."

Herman Rosenfelder frowned and shook his head.

"Kids got no respect nowadays," he said. "A person's got to keep up appearances, Robbie. Half the county was there, and a lot of folks from out East, even a man from the governor's office. Not that they cared a hoot about Alvia, of course, but they all remembered the Senator. Right, Shorty?"

"There was a man!" Shorty Arbuckle agreed.

"Yessir!" Mr. Rosenfelder said. "They don't make 'em like Arthur T. Ivors no more!"

A fire was still smoldering in the stove, as the mornings had been unseasonably cold. The smell of wood smoke mixed pleasantly with the odors of dry goods and horehound and fresh-ground coffee.

"Well," Shorty Arbuckle said, "we'll see some changes around here now."

"High time, if you ask me," Mr. Rosenfelder said. "A woman's got no business runnin' a factory."

"Ain't it the truth, though?" Shorty Arbuckle said. He lowered his voice confidentially. "Mind you now, Alvia Ivors was a fine woman, but I understand she 'n that old housekeeper had regular binges up there!"

"We-ll," Herman Rosenfelder said, "the Herr Doktor'll straighten things out in short order. Heard he's already brought in a new flesher to replace the one Charlie ruint."

"That Charlie!" Shorty Arbuckle said.

"But there's no proof Charlie did it!" Robbie protested.

"No proof?" Mr. Rosenfelder said. "You call runnin' up Hill Street with a gas can in his hand and the tannery in flames behind him no proof? Why, Shorty saw him, didn'tcha, Shorty?"

"For a fact!" Shorty nodded.

38

"Defective, that's what he is," Herman Rosenfelder muttered. He leaned over the cuspidor and spat. "Oughta be in Mendota with his own kind —"

They were still talking when Robbie slipped out the door and started up to the mission to meet Jim.

"Poor Charlie!" Robbie said, later, as he and Jim walked down to the landing to get the canoe. "It seems once they get started, they never let up."

"Aw, old man Rosenfelder don't mean half of what he says, Robbie," Jim said.

"He's a mean old crab, Jim."

"But he's only been that way since his wife died," Jim said. "It's hard when you lose somebody like that."

"Shoot, Jim, that's no excuse for actin' rude," Robbie said, "and runnin' Charlie down that way."

"You got to make allowances, Robbie," Jim said. "My old man used to say if you expect to get an inch in life, be prepared to give two inches."

"You remember that much about your pa, Jim?"

"Shoot, I remember all of it."

"Even the fire?"

"Sure, the fire and crawlin' through the snow and the rangers comin' with their lanterns."

"How'd you feel when you knew your pa was dead?"

"Ever wonder how a dog feels when its master goes off and never comes back?" Jim said. "That's how I felt."

The *Mary Ann,* the launch from Rosenfelder's farm, was tied up at the landing. Robbie noticed a pile of pumpkins in the back of the boat and stared at them in disbelief.

"Will you look at that, Jim!" he fumed, pointing at the pumpkins. "The last week of August and already he's harvestin' his pumpkins! Big ones! Holy cow, he must be a magician! The first pumpkins, the biggest pumpkins, the best pumpkins! . . ."

Jim pulled Robbie into the canoe and laughed all the way across the bay.

8

On Sunday the threat of war seemed to be on everybody's mind.

"The devil is loose over there, boys," Sister Joan Therese said when Robbie stopped by the mission after mass to help Jim with his packing. "The United States has God's work to do."

Jim looked up from the floor where he was sorting things for his footlocker, which would be sent up to Court Oreilles ahead of him on the creamery truck.

"I don't understand, Sister," he said. "D'you mean we should conquer everybody like the Germans are tryin' to do?"

Sister Joan Therese sat on Jim's bed, darning socks. A

flowered apron was wrapped around her black habit, and she wore a dustcap on her head. Robbie had never seen Sister's hair, but he was sure it was white.

"Heavens, no!" Sister exclaimed. "The United States is very special, Jim. The world looks to us to do what's right. I remember how proud I felt when I was in Europe on my pilgrimage. Everybody smiled and made special allowances for you because you were an American and your country did such nice things."

She finished a sock and tossed it to Jim to pack.

"It's a wonderful thing, boys, to be proud of your country and convinced of the integrity of its goals. If only we can control our greed now that hard times are ending. Greed is the undoing of all ages and all nations."

"The Swede says the human race has a flaw," Jim said, "that will destroy us."

"So does the church, Jim," Sister said. "We call it original sin, remember?"

"We-ll, that ain't exactly what the Swede means, Sister," Jim said. "He says man is the only animal that preys on its own kind. He says rabbits don't prey on other rabbits or deer on other deer, but that men prey on men and eventually it will do them in."

"Well!" Sister Joan Therese said with surprise. "It seems the Swede isn't nearly the heathen folks make him out to be."

"Oh, the Swede's not a heathen, Sister," Robbie said. "He's very — well, philosophical, I guess you'd call it. He says Jesus Christ was the only unflawed man in all of history, except for maybe Abraham Lincoln. But he thinks the Indians had the best way of life and probably the best religion too.''

"Does he now?'' Sister said. "And exactly how does he figure that?''

"He says there's no better place to look for God than in the wind and the rain,'' Robbie said, "on account of it's His wind and His rain.''

Sister Joan Therese broke into laughter, a loud, mirthful laughter that made her chin ripple.

"Well!'' she said. "The Holy Father will be pleased to learn that!''

She tossed the last of the socks to Jim, then got to her feet and shook out her habit.

"There, Jim boy,'' she said. "That should hold you for a while. When a boy's got clean socks and clean underwear he can face the world with confidence.''

Jim held his nose and made a noise like a foghorn.

"Beee-ohhh!''

They all laughed. Then Sister turned to Robbie.

"Follow me, Master VanEpp,'' she said, crooking a finger. "We'll take care of your deposition for Charlie Barrow.''

Robbie walked with Sister Joan Therese down the winding brick path that led to the schoolhouse. The old nun's rosary beads clattered in the wind.

"You haven't been to see me all summer,'' she said, reprovingly.

"I've been sort of busy,'' Robbie said.

"Yes, I've heard all about your big plans for the Up Holly. Loon Lodge, isn't it?"

Robbie felt a little surge of pride. "Yes, Sister," he said. "Three hundred and twenty acres. Charlie's going to apply for the homestead in October when he turns twenty-one."

"I assume he won't be applying from the Sawyer County jail," Sister said.

"Shoot, Sister," Robbie said, "Charlie didn't set that fire!"

"I know, Robbie. I just want you to keep a sense of proportion about you. Jim says you were talking about doing yourself in."

Robbie grinned in embarrassment. "That was that day of Alvia's funeral," he said. "I'm okay now."

"Good," Sister said. "For your information, I'm not the least bit concerned about Charlie's trouble. Stanfill P. Stanfill is an honorable man. But — I'm saying a novena just to hedge my bets."

Robbie laughed.

"Now, tell me more about your Loon Lodge."

"Oh-hh, it'll be kind of special, I hope," Robbie said. "We'll market only the very best — vegetables and fruits and jams and syrups. We'll do some manufacturing too, wood products and Indian crafts, and maybe later on we'll start a nursery. It'll be a place where we can raise our families and look after Charlie."

"Heavens!" Sister said. "A veritable dynasty!"

"Not a dynasty, Sister," Robbie said. "Sort of, well,

a tradition, I guess. A place that'll go on for generations and generations."

"And I suppose Livvie Buhl is involved in all this?"

To Robbie's own surprise he felt vaguely bothered by Sister's automatic assumption about Livvie. "In a way," he said, evasively.

"I might have known it," Sister said. "I remember the day you brought her to first-grade, the poor child struggling with that brace and embarrassed to death over her flour-sack underwear. I suspected then the two of you were glued together for life."

They started up the steps of the schoolhouse. The wind gusted up from the bay.

"It's strange," Sister said. "Everybody seems to be scheming to get away from Sister Bay, and here you are scheming to stay. But — life is a process of coming full circle, so perhaps your Loon Lodge will give you a head start."

Robbie braced a foot against the schoolhouse door to keep it from blowing back, then latched it shut behind them. Inside, it was quiet and the rooms were dusty with disuse. May festival decorations still hung from the blackboards.

"Here, Robbie," Sister said, taking down a book from the shelf in her office. "This book will show you the proper form for a deposition. It's the same as an affidavit. Follow the form, but use your own words. Always use your own words!"

Robbie spent the rest of the afternoon at the schoolhouse, helping Sister to unpack books and to rearrange the furniture in her tiny office. It was very pleasant. There was the smell of new books and the sound of the wind outside and the good feeling he always got from Sister's presence. He felt an enduring bond with the old nun. He had known her for as far back as he could remember. She had been an important influence in his life. To experience things together, he was convinced, was the most valuable thing in life. Nothing could destroy the things you shared.

"You'll be having trigonometry this year," Sister said as she walked with Robbie to the door. "If you have any trouble, come see me."

"Yes, Sister," Robbie said.

Robbie walked across the schoolyard and was almost to Silurian Park when Sister Joan Therese called after him.

"Stick to it, Robbie VanEpp! Build your Loon Lodge and be proud of it!"

That night, as he was undressing for bed, something fell from the pocket of Robbie's trousers. It was the envelope from Mrs. Armitage. He opened the envelope, took out the two one-dollar bills it contained and was about to throw it in the wastebasket when he noticed a little piece of paper. It was a note from Mrs. Armitage.

It was important that she find Alvia's Pinafore box, she had written. She had searched Moonrise from top to bottom before she left but to no avail. There had been strange goings-on the week before Alvia died, she said. The Herr Doktor had come over, and he and Alvia had argued bitterly. The next day Alvia had sneaked off on the train down to Eau Claire or Chippewa Falls, she wasn't sure which —

Robbie's heart quickened when he came to the last paragraph.

    . . . I think she made out a new will, Robbie, and hid it in her Pinafore box. The only place I haven't looked is Billy Sashabaw's lake. She had a strange attachment to that place. Go to Billy Sashabaw's lake, Robbie. You were her friend. Go to Billy Sashabaw's lake! . . .

9

Sister Bay had had several lives, first as an Indian trading post, then as a thriving fur center, and later, after the railroad came, as a bawdy sawmill town. The old-timers liked to boast that Radisson and Groseilliers had come down Big Chetac in 1654, but there was no proof of it, and besides, the Chippewas had roamed the wooded hills for centuries before the *voyageurs,* hunting the Flambeau and fishing the Narrows and tapping the tall maples for golden syrup. The bay seemed naturally to attract commerce, sheltered as it was by the bluffs and the pine-covered headlands where it opened on the lake.

The Chippewas said you could canoe up Big Chetac and then follow the rivers and streams all the way to the big lake, Lake Superior. Robbie had never tried it, but he was familiar with the maze of little lakes that lay beyond Big Chetac and the many creeks that flowed out of them. One of them, Knuteson Creek, branched off from the lower arm of Big Chetac and led to a tiny lake in the wilderness about four miles due east of Moonrise. On the maps the lake was listed as Wise Lake, but to Alvia Ivors it had always been Billy Sashabaw's lake, so named after the itinerant Winnebago trapper who had once saved her life.

"Alvia was about twelve when it happened," Robbie explained to Livvie and Jim the next morning. "She's got her legs all scratched up in those brambles above the Narrows, and blood poisoning set in —"

He and Jim had canoed up to Buhl Farm at dawn, before the wind started whipping up, and now they were sitting around the kitchen table while Livvie packed them all a lunch.

" — Anyway, the infection spread above her knees. Ol' Doc Davies told the Senator he'd have to amputate. The Senator was fit to be tied. He swore at Doc Davies and called him a dumb quack, and then he hopped the *Limited* down to Chicago to bring up some specialists. That's when Billy Sashabaw showed up — "

"Was he a friend of the Senator's?" Livvie asked.

"Shoot, he'd been driftin' in and out of Moonrise for years," Robbie said, "doin' odd jobs and stuff. Anyway, Billy lanced Alvia's legs and soaked them overnight in a mash he'd made of fresh-dug potatoes. By morning the poison was all drained away. The Senator was so grateful, he gave Billy the run of the place, and Alvia tagged after him like he was her father.''

"I keep forgettin'," Jim said. "Alvia was an orphan too, wasn't she?''

"Even worse than you, Jim," Robbie said. "She had no memory of her parents at all. She was still in her cradle when her ma and pa died.''

"Yeah," Jim said. "I guess it ain't all peaches and cream, is it? Even when you're the Senator's granddaughter and live in a fancy place like Moonrise.''

"Whatever happened to Billy Sashabaw?" Livvie asked.

"Alvia never said, Livvie," Robbie said. "I guess later on there were hard feelings between Billy and the Senator. You see, Billy used to take Alvia over to that lake and teach her the old Indian rituals. The Senator accused him of bein' a bad influence on her, but Mrs. Armitage said that deep down he was really jealous of Billy. Anyhow, I guess he just drifted off.''

They were silent for a few minutes. Then Jim made a face and shook his head.

"People sure can mess each other up," he said, "can't they?''

It was agreed they would go to Billy Sashabaw's lake on foot. The blow was moving in, and Big Chetac would be too rough for the canoe.

"What does Alvia's Pinafore box look like, Robbie?" Livvie asked, slipping into a sweater.

"It's just a regular music box, Livvie," Robbie said, "like somethin' you'd keep jewelry in. There's a drawing of some Gilbert and Sullivan characters on the lid. That's why she called it her Pinafore box."

"Are there any totems over there, Robbie?" Jim said. "Totems make good hiding places."

"There's an old Indian camp," Robbie said, "but everything's rotted away."

"Then where on earth could she have hidden anything?" Livvie asked.

"There's an old hollowed-out stump, Livvie," Robbie replied. "She used to keep a lot of private stuff in the stump."

They hiked up past Hauger's Landing and then around the northern tip of Big Chetac. It was dense woods most of the way, hardwoods at first and then pines, great towering pines that made them dizzy when they looked up at them. The pines kept the floor of the forest moist and cool and soft underfoot. Jim led the way surely and steadily, marking a trail to guide them on the way back. The heavy weather was settling in, and the wind howled through the trees.

"She's blowin'!" Jim called out in glee, clutching his hat with one hand. "Ooo-eee!"

Robbie held his head high in the wind and breathed deeply. It was as if the sharp, piercing gusts were a kind of absolution that was cleansing his mind of the troubled thoughts of the past week. In three more days it would be September, and there would be cider and doughnuts in the roadside stands. It would be a fine autumn, he thought, and a fine winter. The snow would come early, in swirling blue-gray squalls, clinging to the trees cold and clean and pure. February would be the worst; the Swede said nature settled her accounts in February. Then just when you thought you couldn't stand another minute of it, the crocuses would break through like watercolors spilled in the snow. It was a fine arrangement, he thought. Every year winter would come — and go. And spring and summer and autumn. But autumn, somehow, was best. It was pretty in the autumn. The forest turned red and gold, and the special smells did something to your thinking.

"Look, Jim!" They were crossing a little brook, and Livvie had spotted a moose, a huge bull, splashing about upstream. "Isn't he a beauty?"

She kicked off her shoes to wade up for a closer look. As she did so, the collar of her dress caught a thorn, and there was a loud tearing sound. Jim pulled her back.

"Stay here, Livvie!" he whispered. "He'll charge you."

They hunched down in the brush until the moose loped out of the stream and disappeared in the woods.

"He probably strayed away from the herd," Jim said. "I hope the wolf packs don't get him."

"Wolf packs!" Livvie exclaimed.

"They prey on moose, Livvie," Jim explained. "Usually they try to pick off the calves or stragglers that are weak or sick."

"Golly!" Livvie whispered, a little shiver running

52

through her. "Maybe there's wolves lurkin' about right now."

"Maybe," Jim said. "But the wolves won't hurt you. The moose will, but the wolves won't."

The sun was nearly straight up when they came out on a clearing atop the line of hills that rimmed Billy Sashabaw's lake. It was a small, narrow lake, barely a hundred yards across in places, bordered by tall white pines. The trees shut out the sun and gave the lake a desolate, almost eerie quality. Along the shore the trunks of rotted trees angled up out of the water, and the cry of the loon was everywhere.

"Golly!" Livvie said. "It's so spooky!"

"The Chippewas always picked spooky places, Livvie," Jim said. "They're better for spirits."

They flopped down to catch their breath. They were all very tired, a nice kind of tiredness. To the west, there was a lovely view of Big Chetac. The turreted roof of Moonrise glinted in the sun.

"Whereabouts is that Indian camp, Robbie?" Jim said.

"Just below us," Robbie said. "You can't see it from here."

Jim walked to the edge of the clearing to inspect the terrain leading down to the lake, and then suddenly dropped to his knees and made a warning signal with his arms. Robbie and Livvie scrambled over on their elbows.

"What is it, Jim?" Robbie whispered.

Jim pointed down at the lake. Three men on horseback were moving out of the clearing where the Indian camp had been and were turning onto the trail leading back to Moonrise.

"Holy cow!" Livvie whispered. "It's the Herr Doktor!"

The horses broke into a trot, with the Herr Doktor in the lead. He was a small man who carried himself in an erect, haughty manner, like a toy soldier, and thus seemed taller than he actually was.

"Who're the other two guys, Robbie?" Jim said.

"Edgar Bauer," Robbie said, "and Earl Dodson. He was Alvia's attorney till she fired him."

The horses went out of sight up the trail.

"What d'you think they're up to, Jim?" Robbie said.

"Beats me."

"Look!" Livvie said. "There's a boat pulled up at the clearing."

It was the *Arthur T.*, the tannery launch, a twenty-footer with a little wheel house up front and swivel chairs for the passengers. The big schooner bell in the bow flashed in the sun like a heliograph.

"C'mon," Jim said, getting to his feet. "Let's poke around."

The *Arthur T.* was still beached in the clearing when they started for home. The excursion had been a failure. The hollowed-out stump had proved empty, save for a slim volume of poetry, a lace handkerchief, and a half-full bottle of gin, which Robbie covered with leaves so that Jim and Livvie wouldn't see.

54

"What d'you make of it, Jim?" Robbie said as they crossed back over the brook where they had seen the moose.

"I don't know, Robbie," Jim said. "Maybe there's nothin' to it. Maybe the Herr Doktor just wanted to talk business with Edgar Bauer, him bein' manager of the tannery 'n all."

"Funny way to come visitin'," Robbie said, "up Knuteson Creek to Billy Sashabaw's lake and then four miles on horseback. And what about Mr. Dodson?"

"Robbie's right, Jim," Livvie said. "It looks fishy, if you ask me."

It was dusk by the time they came back around the tip of Big Chetac. The wind had died down. A misty gray light filtered through the trees as through a church window at twilight. When they came out on the path that led down to Hauger's Landing, they spotted a tall figure with a lantern looming out of the shadows.

"Halloo!" a voice boomed out. "That you, Robbie?"

"It's the Swede!" Robbie said. "Halloo, Swede!"

The Swede's sunburned face glowed brightly in the lantern light.

"Shake a tail," he said when he came up on them. "We're goin' up to see Charlie tonight."

"Oh, swell!" Livvie cried. "Let's take him something to eat."

"We saw Edgar Bauer and the Herr Doktor over at Billy Sashabaw's lake, Swede," Robbie said. "Somethin' fishy's goin' on."

"We'll worry 'bout the Herr Doktor tomorrow, Robbie," the Swede said. "Livvie, you'd best fix your dress 'fore we get back."

Livvie blushed. "Golly," she giggled, "I forgot."

Jim and the Swede started down the path. Livvie hung behind while Robbie fixed the clasp she's snagged on the thorn. It made Robbie feel good the way Livvie had automatically turned to him to fix her dress.

"You'll have to lift up your sweater, Livvie," he said.

As he worked the clasp, Robbie's fingers slipped under Livvie's shift and brushed over her bare shoulder. Her skin felt soft and warm. Livvie turned to face him.

"Pretty soon it will be our time, Robbie," she said, putting her arms around him.

Robbie could feel Livvie's hard little breasts pressing against his chest. There was a tingling sensation deep in him somewhere, the same sensation he always felt when he hooked a fish and knew it was a big one.

"We'll just let it happen," Livvie whispered. She stood on her toes and kissed him lightly on the lips. "It's important to just let things happen." And then she turned and ran down the path after Jim and the Swede.

They hiked single-file down the lake, the good sounds and good smells of the woods all around them, the Swede leading the way and Jim and Livvie silhouetted behind him in the glow of the lantern.

Robbie felt very happy. They had been to the wilderness, and now they were back. It was a fine feeling.

10

There was a bright moon as the Swede rattled his old pickup up Iowa Street in Hayward and turned off at the courthouse. Livvie sat up front with the Swede. Robbie and Jim rode in back, their legs dangling down over the cobblestone streets and the night air cool on their faces.

"Gives you a funny feelin', don't it?" Jim said. "Visitin' somebody who's in jail."

Robbie seldom got to go up to Hayward, except at Christmastime when the Holy Childhood choir sang carols in the square. It was lovely then, with holly strung everywhere and turkeys hanging in the window of Olmsted's butcher shop and the stores all lit up. But now the streets were dark and deserted, and the courthouse loomed ominously in the shadows.

"We should've brought the sign," Robbie said. "The sign might boost Charlie's spirits."

The jail was in the rear wing of the courthouse. There was an office downstairs and a narrow circular stairway, like a spiral, that led up to the cells. The deputy, a pudgy little man in a worn khaki uniform, saw the Swede's truck pull up and came out on the porch to greet them.

" 'Evenin', Swede," he said. "Thought youse wasn't goin' to make it. Violet and her mother are just leavin'."

"She sober?" the Swede said.

"Mrs. Barrow?" the deputy said. He grinned. "Barely."

They started into the jail. The deputy noticed Jim coming up the steps.

"The Indian'll have to wait out here," he said to the Swede.

"But Jim's our friend," Robbie protested.

"Sorry, Robbie," the deputy said. "Sheriff's orders. No redskins allowed." And then he laughed. "Less'n they're prisoners, of course."

"But that ain't fair!" Robbie said.

Jim nudged him. "It don't matter, Robbie," he said. "I'll wait in the truck."

Jim started down the steps, tight-lipped, his black hat shoved down over his eyes. Robbie felt a terrible shame well up in him.

58

"For cryin' out loud — " he began, but Livvie took his arm.

"It'll be all right, Robbie," she whispered. "Maybe Charlie can wave to Jim through the window."

The deputy led them through a little anteroom with a wooden bench and a spittoon.

"We let Charlie have the run of the place durin' the day," he said to the Swede. "That way we can keep an eye on him in case he has a spell."

Charlie's mother and his sister Violet were coming down the stairs.

"Robbie!" Mrs. Barrow cried out. "Livvie!" She gave the two of them wet kisses. There was a faint odor of gin about her.

"Come on, Mama," Violet said. "You'll fall down."

"My Charlie's got good friends, Violet," Mrs. Barrow said. Her eyes were red from crying. "They won't let him down."

Violet sighed impatiently. "Yes, Mama," she said.

Violet Barrow looked thin and tired, in a plain cotton dress and the tennis shoes, with anklets, that she wore to ease her feet against the hard floors at the Dew Drop Inn. Everybody said she would end up an old maid the way she wore herself out looking after her mother and Charlie.

"Are they going to send Charlie to Mendota, Violet?" Livvie said.

"I don't know, Livvie," Violet replied. "It's all so complicated."

59

Mrs. Barrow mussed up Robbie's hair.

"Are you goin' to take Charlie fishin' in the Narrows, Robbie?"

"Yes, ma'am," Robbie said. "First chance we get."

"That'll be nice, Robbie," Mrs. Barrow smiled. "Charlie likes fishin' the Narrows." And then her voice trailed off in a whisper. "His papa used to row me up there in the springtime. Everything was so fresh and lovely — "

Violet took Mrs. Barrow's arm. "Come on, Mama," she said. "You're tired."

The deputy helped Violet with her mother. They started for the door.

"We're goin' to Belgium next week, Robbie," Mrs. Barrow called back, "to put flowers on Mr. Barrow's grave. It's not right for him to be in Belgium. There are no hills and the nights are damp — "

There was a little commotion when they got out on the porch.

"Swede?" the deputy called inside. "You'd best give me a hand. Tell the kids they can go on up if they want."

Robbie and Livvie went upstairs alone. Livvie took Robbie's hand and held it tight.

"I'm scared, Robbie!" she whispered.

The jail consisted of a row of six cells that opened on a low-ceilinged corridor. A single light bulb provided the only light, making it difficult to see. The cells were all alike, a wooden bunk, a pail of water, a chamber pot. A drunken Chippewa was sprawled face-down on the floor in one of the cells. There was the smell of fish and vomit and cheap whiskey.

"Oh, it's awful!" Livvie said, shivering. "Poor Charlie!"

The door of the last cell was ajar. They could make out a form sitting Indian-fashion in the corner of the bunk. It was Charlie. He peered out at them uncertainly, his head twitching slightly.

"R-r-robbie?" he whispered, his eyes wide. "L-l-livvie?"

"Hello, Charlie," Robbie said. "We brought you some cheese and sausage."

Charlie managed a little grin.

"Hey, h-h-hey on the midway!" he said, weakly, his voice hoarse and his arms windmilling a little as he struggled to get up.

"Oh, Charlie, Charlie, Charlie!" Livvie cried, jumping up and down. "I thought the jail would make you different, but it hasn't!"

They piled into Charlie's bunk, talking all at once, with the jailhouse mattress dirty and stained and the drunken Chippewa moaning from up the corridor.

"How are they treating you, Charlie?" Livvie said.

"Sh-sh-shoot," he said, "it's a regular ho-ho-hotel."

They broke into raucous laughter.

Robbie grinned happily. It was the sticking together, he was convinced. Nothing could hurt you if you stuck together.

11

There was something in Indian Jim that was shut off from Robbie. It was an anger, perhaps, or a great sadness. It showed in his eyes when he spoke of Court Oreilles, and it showed whenever he was insulted because of his race. The Swede said all Indians were sad, that it had been bred into them by four centuries of hardship and betrayal.

Jim was in one of his dark moods on the drive back down to Sister Bay. Robbie knew he had been hurt by the business with the deputy.

"I'll bet if Mr. Stanfill was sheriff," Robbie said, "Indians would be allowed to visit at the jail."

Jim laughed sarcastically.

"I'm beginnin' to think that's what's wrong with the world," he said. "There's not enough Stanfill P. Stanfills to go around."

They fell into silence. The night was bright and clear. The road wound through a valley of scraggy little farms, some of them abandoned, set back against the hills that bordered Court Oreilles. Nobody knew much about the families that worked them. Starve-to-death farms, the Swede called them, on account of the soil was rocky and sandy and the spring thaws left deep gullies in the fields. The silos and broken windmills made forlorn silhouettes against the star-filled sky. Robbie pointed to the charred remains of a shack that had burned to the ground.

"If Loon Lodge don't work out," he said to Jim, "maybe we could fix that place up."

Jim looked and grinned. "Too rich for my blood," he said.

Jim slouched glumly against the side of the truck, his knees drawn up against his chest. It disturbed Robbie to see his friend hurt and upset. A special kinship existed between him and Jim, Robbie was convinced, a kind of predestination that went back to the night they were both born. There was a legend in the VanEpp family about that night, about how his mother had been frightened by a black bear on the way home from the Friday fish fry at Andy's Tavern, and Robbie had been born four hours later, in the big front bedroom. They said Nate VanEpp had got so excited, he skidded Gramps' new Overland into a ditch below Hauger's Landing. The Swede had had to take them back to town in the *Ruby Allen* with Nate Van-Epp holding a lantern to light the way through the Narrows. The Swede was a young man then and just starting out as a cheese maker.

Nobody had been aware of it at the time, but as the *Ruby Allen* was winding through the Narrows, Jim was being born in a shanty up on the reservation. The Northern Lights came out that night. Gramps said it was a good omen.

It was funny about different races, Robbie thought. The Bible said God had made people that way as a punishment, but the Swede said it was on account of the climate. People in Africa were black, he said, because their skin had to filter out certain rays of the sun that could be harmful if you got too much of them. It was just the opposite in Norway and Sweden, he said, and so people up there were white. Robbie knew the Swede was right. That's why white people looked out of place in the Congo and black people looked out of place in the snow. It was different with Indians; Indians looked like a part of the land everywhere.

Robbie had been up to Court Oreilles only once, when he was a small boy, but he had never forgotten it. He had expected it to be a grand place with tepees and pretty maidens and handsome Chippewa braves on spotted ponies. But it wasn't that way at all. It was tarpaper shanties, junk Model T's, dirty kids sucking on watermelon rinds, a lot of Indian men drunk and passed out, and everywhere a funny smell. Life was hard on the reservation, Jim said, and in the winter many people died.

But Robbie had never thought of Jim as being a part of the reservation and the shanties. Jim was different. Jim was smart and handsome and knew how to get on with folks. Still, Jim was an Indian; there was no changing that. And Robbie wondered if they were approaching a time when Jim's Indian-ness would affect their friendship.

"Robbie?" Jim said as the truck wound down out of a hill and Big Chetac came into view below them.

"Yeah, Jim?"

"We're really blood brothers, aren't we?"

"We sure are, Jim boy."

"It's not just bull, is it?" Jim said. "So many things are bull."

"Oh, we're blood brothers all right, Jim," Robbie said. "Forever and ever."

"You think we'll ever build our place on the Up Holly?"

"Of course we'll build it, Jim. Haven't we got the sign all ready to put up? And didn't Charlie write to Madison for the homestead application the week before the fire?"

"Shoot, you wrote that letter, Robbie. Charlie's hands shake too much."

"Well, what's the difference?" Robbie said. "Charlie signed it, didn't he?"

"When we were in sixth grade," Jim said, "we were going to build a raft to float down the Narrows. We talked of it all year, but we never did it."

"Yeah, but this is different, Jim."

"What if they put Charlie in Mendota?" Jim said. "Who'll apply for the homestead then? Your pa thinks it's all a big joke, and the Swede ain't eligible on account of he's already had one homestead."

"There's Livvie's pa. He's never had one. Their farm was private land when they bought it."

"You know we can't ask him, Robbie. You said yourself it wouldn't be right."

"No, it wouldn't," Robbie said. "Well, then I guess we'd just have to wait till you'n me turn twenty-one."

"But that's four years," Jim said. "A lot can happen in four years."

"Don't be so gloomy, Jim," Robbie said. "They won't send Charlie to Mendota."

"Well, what if your pa lands a job while he's down in Chicago? What then?"

Robbie laughed. "Shoot, Jim," he said, "Dad's been talkin' of gettin' a job down there for as long as I can remember, but he never has, 'cept for that time at the world's fair."

"But do you really think we'll do it?" Jim persisted. "Do you really think we'll build Loon Lodge?"

Jim was making Robbie uneasy.

"Holy mackerel, Jim boy! What's got into you anyway?"

Jim took off his hat to keep it from blowing away. The red cardinal feather gleamed in the moonlight.

"Shoot, I don't know, Robbie," he said. "It's just that

everything seems to be slippin' away from us. D'you know what I mean?''

Robbie looked down at the lake. The *Arthur T.* was heading out from Hauger's Landing on its final run of the night.

"Yeah, Jim boy," he said, his voice lost on the wind. "I know what you mean."

12

Later that night, back at the Swede's, with a fire crackling against the chill and everybody drawn up around it with platters of bratwurst and cheese and baked beans, Robbie thought of the vomit smell of the jail and felt ashamed of his ravenous appetite.

" — But I don't see why they can't let Charlie out on bail or something," Livvie was saying as she came in from the kitchen carrying a tray with a pail of Old Style Lager for the Swede and mugs of hot cocoa for Robbie and Jim. "Golly, they don't even bother to lock his cell."

"It was Stan's idea to keep him in jail, Livvie," the

68

Swede said. "The tannery was shut down on account of that fire. Folks're resentful over the lost wages, and Stan don't want them takin' it out on Charlie."

The Swede filled his stein from the pail. Outside, the shutters rattled noisily as the blow moved steadily down from the north.

"Why can't Mr. Stanfill just drop the charges," Jim said, "and let Charlie go?"

"It ain't that simple, Jim," the Swede said. "There's folks to be got off the hook — Edgar Bauer who signed the complaint, and the deputy who made the arrest, and Shorty Arbuckle who signed a statement implicatin' Charlie."

"Shoot," Jim said, "what's all that got to do with it?"

"For most folks, Jim," the Swede said, "that's what life's all about, gettin' off the hook. So if you're figurin' to keep Charlie out of Mendota, you'd best find somebody to take his place up in that cell."

Robbie listened in silence. There was a system to things, he was discovering. The system was a collection of jobs. It seemed anything could be justified, even sending Charlie to Mendota, so long as it was your job.

"What I can't figure out," Jim said, "is what Charlie was doin' with that gas can."

"He was runnin' up to town hall to turn in the alarm, Jim," Livvie said. "He'd found the can back in the fleshing-room where the fire started."

"Shoot," Jim said, "why didn't he just phone the alarm?"

"The way Charlie stutters?" Livvie said.

They all laughed.

Robbie mulled over what Charlie had told them up in the jail. He had shown up to sweep out the tannery offices at the usual time, he had said. It had been no different from any other day, except for one thing: Normally, Edgar Bauer stayed till Charlie was finished in order to lock up, but on the day of the fire he left word that he had some errands to run and for Charlie to lock up and leave the key at Hugo's.

" — But it just don't seem fair, Swede," Jim was saying.

" 'Course it ain't fair, Jim," the Swede said. "Nothin' about life is fair, and don't you ever forget it. Make a sampler out of it and tack it on the wall along with the Golden Rule and 'Home Sweet Home.' 'Life Ain't Fair.' "

He took a long drink from his stein and wiped his mouth on the back of his hand.

"So stop carpin' about how it ain't fair and start figurin' out who really set that fire." He turned to Robbie. "Robbie, you got any notions who the culprit might be, or cul*prits,* for that matter?"

And in that moment it all became clear to Robbie.

"The Herr Doktor," he said, "and Edgar Bauer."

The Swede started to laugh, then thought better of it.

"Mr. Dodson was probably in on it too," Robbie said. "Alvia said he was out to skin her."

"By golly," the Swede said, "I think he's serious."

70

"But why would they do it, Robbie?" Livvie said. "There'd have to be a motive."

"Shoot," Robbie said, "a dozen reasons, probably. Everybody knew the Herr Doktor was anglin' to buy out Alvia at the tannery. Mrs. Armitage said he wanted Moonrise so bad he could taste it."

"But," Stan said, "the Herr Doktor was out of town that day, Robbie," the Swede said, "and that Edgar Bauer was up at Hugo's havin' a beer."

"They didn't have to be there, Swede," Robbie explained. "With those candles and the excelsior we found in the launch and maybe an open pan of gasoline they could make a regular time bomb."

"Well, I'll be danged!" the Swede said. "It makes sense. It makes real good sense!"

Livvie and Jim leaped to their feet and began dancing around.

"That's it, Robbie!" Livvie cried. "That's it! Oh, wait till we tell Charlie!"

The Swede calmed them down.

"Now don't go tellin' a soul, Livvie," he said, "least of all Charlie. Solvin' it is one thing, but provin' it is a horse of a different color. There's still all that evidence against Charlie."

"What should we do, Swede?" Jim asked.

The Swede reached forward to poke up the fire. A flurry of sparks showered onto the fieldstone hearth.

"We'll just sit tight, Jim," he said, "till we talk to Stanfill P. Stanfill."

"What about Alvia's Pinafore box?" Jim said. "I guess it don't matter much now, does it?"

" 'Course it does, Jim boy," the Swede said. "It matters more'n ever. Stan ain't goin' to arrest the Herr Doktor just on our say-so. Besides, Robbie owes it to Alvia and Mrs. Armitage. It's a matter of right and wrong."

"I'll bet the Herr Doktor's already found the will," Livvie said, "and torn it up."

"Maybe, Livvie," the Swede said, "and then again, maybe not." He drained his stein and got to his feet. "Well, we'd best sleep on it for a bit. C'mon, Livvie, I'll run you down to the farm."

Livvie slipped into her sweater and got ready to leave.

"Oh, I just know everything's goin' to be all right," she said. "We'll get Charlie out of that awful jail, and then maybe the town will feel so bad they'll take up a collection so that Mrs. Barrow can visit her husband's grave in Belgium like she's always wanted."

"Her husband ain't buried in Belgium, Livvie," the Swede said.

Livvie looked up, puzzled.

"But I don't understand, Swede."

"He ain't buried at all, Livvie. He's sellin' ties in Passaic, New Jersey."

"You mean he wasn't killed in the war?" Jim said.

"Nope," the Swede said. "The farthest he ever got with the American Expeditionary Force was Camp Kilmer, and then he ran off with some girl from the Red Cross canteen."

"Holy cow!" Jim said. "Don't Mrs. Barrow know he's alive?"

"Oh, she knows it all right, Jim," the Swede said. "She just shut her mind to it."

The wind blew back the screen door as they went outside. Waves were breaking hard against the boathouse where the Swede kept the *Ruby Allen*. They started up past the smokehouse to the truck, Livvie leading the way. The wind swept back her hair and blew her dress tight against her legs. Robbie pulled out his shirt and let the wind gust over his bare skin. It felt good and clean.

"Looks like it's goin' to be a swell blow, Swede," he said.

"Yah, Robbie," the Swede said, a little unsteady on his feet after all the beer. "It'll be a fine blow all right."

13

Livvie Buhl lay awake very late that night. Sleep wouldn't come. There was so much to think about, Charlie's mother and the Herr Doktor and that sweet moment with Robbie in the woods.

The old farmhouse creaked in the wind. The night was friendly. The trees rustled outside, and the moon made shadows on the flowered wallpaper.

Livvie tossed and turned for what seemed hours. Finally, she threw off the feather comforter and crossed the room to the closet. A long mirror hung on the inside of the closet door. Livvie lit a lamp and let her long cotton nightgown fall to the floor. She stood back and ran her hands over her small breasts. If only she were tanned all over, but maybe in the soft light of the loft it wouldn't matter. She wondered what her mother had looked like at sixteen. Farm ladies seemed destined to grow stout and chalky and sit on the porch in rockers. It was the season of things, she supposed. A season to be tanned and slender, a season to be stout and chalky.

She held her right leg forward, turning it to inspect it from all angles. The deformity was scarcely noticeable. You had to know it was there to detect the slight withering below the knee. It had been worth it, she thought, those long months in the hospital.

She slipped the nightgown over her head, blew out the lamp and crawled back into bed. The wind came in the window, and the sound of waves breaking on the pier carried up from the landing. It was the one nice thing to come of it, she thought, having the big corner bedroom for her own. Her thoughts went back to that hot August day she had clambered down from the *Limited* with her brothers, Ernest and Howard, feverish and oddly exhilarated, after a week at Aunt Bea's in Milwaukee.

"It's just the excitement of the trip, Henry," Lela Buhl had assured her husband. "Lands, the child's only five years old, and she's never set foot out of Sawyer County before! She'll be just fine after a good night's sleep in her own bed."

Livvie couldn't get over the remarkable clarity of her perceptions, and that night when she saw the moon, framed in the window of her bedroom, it was as if she could climb up on it, if only she could get a ladder over to where it came up, in the hills behind Moonrise. She would grab hold and ride round the universe, and afterwards Robbie and Jim would carry her up Main Street on their shoulders. *"That's the Buhl kid!"* the farm ladies would whisper at Arbuckle's. *"A regular Flash Gordon!"* And maybe Raymond Gram Swing would come to Sister Bay to interview her on the radio.

"All the world is waiting, Livvie! Tell us, what is the moon really like?"

"It's soft and cool, like orange sherbet, and there are no mosquitoes."

They had found her out near the barn, tangled in the stepladder, delirious and with a terrible pain spreading through her body. She kept begging her father to move her from bed to bed, as if the coolness of fresh sheets might make the pain go away, but just a twitch of a finger and it would start up again.

The delirium lasted for a week.

"Where's Ernest?" she asked on the seventh day. "Where's Howard?"

But Ernest and Howard were dead; the virus had struck them in the lungs and paralyzed their breathing. And three weeks later Livvie lay crippled in the big hospital down in Madison. It was a strange disease. All she knew of it was that every January Mr. Roosevelt gave a grand ball and the money went to help the children in the iron lungs. She couldn't understand why she was still alive. She couldn't understand why she wasn't in an iron lung like the children in Ward B. She didn't know why she was sick. It was the city, mama kept saying. There were germs in the city.

They had loved her at the hospital. The nurses, Mrs. Archibald and Miss MacLaine, brought her horehound and puzzles, and Dr. Murray, a tall gruff man who smelled of pipe tobacco, worked with her every day in hydrotherapy.

"And how's our little Nanook of the North today?" he would boom. "Now, now, none of that sniveling! We'll have you mushing through the woods again in no time. But you've got to work hard at it. You've got to work very hard."

It was lonely in the hospital. She missed the lake; she missed the woods. Then one day the Swede brought Robbie and Jim down to see her. Livvie fought back the tears.

"Can I still fish the Up Holly with you?" she said, anxiously. "Even though I can't walk?"

"Sure, Livvie," Jim said. "We'll do everything together, same's before."

Robbie handed her an awkwardly wrapped package.

"We got it at Arbuckle's, Livvie," he said. "It's a journal. You know, like a ship's log."

"Yeah," Jim said. "Dr. Murray said you should make a record of how far you can move your leg. The nurses will teach you how to write."

Livvie was certain she was experiencing the happiest moment of her life.

"Oh, it's the swellest present I ever got!" she cried, reaching up to hug them. "I'll write in it every day for the rest of my life! Cross my heart!"

77

Ten months later, it was time to leave.

"We've done all we can for you, Livvie," Dr. Murray said. "Now it's up to you. It won't be easy, but just remember this: Everybody is handicapped in one form or another; yours shows, that's all."

They had let her go home alone on the *Limited*. It was a lovely ride, through rolling green farmland, rich and sweet-smelling and bursting with crops. Guernseys and Holsteins lazed in the pastures, and dust clouded up from country roads. Then, farther north, the land rose in shale cliffs and pine plateaus, and countless lakes and rivers and streams glittered like emeralds in the sun. It was nice, she thought, to come from a state you could be proud of, so clean and green and rich and beautiful it made you ache. Even being crippled couldn't take your state away from you. Your state was strong and lovely. It would soothe your hurts and look after you.

There was an anxious moment when the train rounded Thunder Ridge and started its run down to the bay. Livvie wanted to lock herself in the rest room and ride the *Limited* forever. But then she saw them — Mama, Papa, the Swede, Mr. and Mrs. VanEpp, and up on a baggage cart, Robbie and Jim clowning around and making faces. She stumbled and dropped a crutch, but it didn't matter.

"We're fishin' the Narrows tomorrow, Livvie," Robbie said. "The Swede fixed up a special seat for you in the *Ruby Allen*."

"Yeah," Jim said. "We spotted Ol' Sawtooth up there

yesterday. We figure we'll use a minnow for bait and boat him with a big net — ''

None of it mattered, the pain, the brace, the withered leg. She was home.

14

By morning the blow was at gale force. The wind flattened the bulrushes, and there were dark menacing waves with whitecaps that looked like foam.

Robbie was up early. Jim and the Swede were still asleep. He slipped out of the Swede's cabin and walked down to the lake. He had been looking forward to the autumn windstorms and was glad they had come early. Certain weather, he had learned, was good for certain thoughts. Storms were good for solitude, for thinking things through.

He thought of the jail and wondered if Charlie would have a good breakfast. It had all seemed so simple last night, keeping Charlie out of Mendota, but now he wasn't so sure. Things always looked different in the morning. At night solutions came easy, but in the morning it was different.

He looked up the lake toward the Up Holly and thought of what Jim had said about Loon Lodge. Maybe Jim was right; maybe it was all a pipe dream, even without Charlie's difficulties. Maybe circumstances defeated you if you bit off too much. Maybe that was what had happened on those scraggy little farms up in the valley, with the barns half blown away and stumps sticking up in the pastures. On Saturday nights you would see the farmers stumbling out of Hugo's saloon, talking dirty and their eyes red from too much Old Style Lager. They all seemed alike, those scraggy farmers, the same deep creases in their necks, the same dirty kids asleep out in the pickup, the same worried wives finagling to stretch their credit at Arbuckle's. And you would look at them and wonder how it had been for them when they were young. Maybe they had been like him and Livvie. Maybe circumstances had defeated them.

He remembered the time in eighth grade when a duststorm had blown up from the Southwest. Great clouds of dust had shut out the sun and made the sky an eerie greenish-black. They had had to light the lamps in order to see the blackboard.

"Jesus, Mary, and Joseph!" Sister Joan Therese had whispered in disbelief. "Oklahoma is blowing away!"

It was from the Dust Bowl, she had explained. There had been a bad drought, and the soil had got cropped out.

Thousands of families had lost their farms and were wandering the roads. Later, she had led the class into church and lit a candle under the statue of the Virgin Mary.

"Pray for the homeless wanderers, children!"

Maybe a person got cropped out too, Robbie thought. Maybe in the end it all blew away in dust, your hopes and dreams, your Loon Lodges.

He turned from the lake and started back up to the house. The trees swayed in the wind. It was funny, he thought, how things were never the way you thought they would be. All his life his greatest satisfaction had been in doing things, in hooking a musky or tracking a deer or building a birch-bark canoe. The achievement itself was unimportant; it was the doing that mattered. That was the challenge of Loon Lodge, the doing of it for its own sake. But now it was beginning to seem terribly complicated. He thought of what Livvie had said in the woods and felt a lovely excitement, but a resentment too. Livvie was crowding him.

"You'd best leave the canoe here," the Swede said when Robbie got back up to the house, "and hike back to town."

"Shoot, we can make it okay," Jim said. "We'll stick close to shore and then portage around the Narrows."

The kitchen was filled with good smells, sausages and eggs and the Swede's special potatoes, which he fixed with chopped onions and crumbled bacon and fried till there was a brown crust on them. They sat at the table and ate and talked. There was no mention of Charlie.

"You'll be leavin' for the reservation soon," the Swede said, "won't you, Jim?"

Jim nodded and reached for another sausage. "The night of the potluck, Swede." The sausage made a popping noise when he bit into it. "I'm ridin' up on the milk train."

"This'll be your last year at the Federal school," the Swede said. "Made any plans for after graduation?"

Jim shrugged. "Dig worms, probably," he said, "unless I can get on at the tannery. 'Course if we could get started on Loon Lodge — "

"We-ll, Jim boy, I've been thinkin'." The Swede stuck a toothpick in his mouth and leaned back in his chair. "There's a broker down in Milwaukee claims if the war situation gets any worse he'll be able to sell all the cheese I can make, and sausages too. I figure I could maybe double my output, providin' I had a little help round here."

Jim's face lit up. "You mean you'd hire me?"

"Why not?" the Swede said. "A town's got to look after its own, don't it? We could fix you a place of your own out in the shed, and there'd be plenty of time for Loon Lodge."

Jim let out a whoop.

"Holy cow, Swede, that'd be swell!" He thumped his feet excitedly on the floor. "Gee, wait'll I tell Sister Joan Therese!"

"Now don't go countin' your chickens 'fore they're hatched, Jim boy," the Swede cautioned, and then turned to Robbie and winked. " 'Course it probably wouldn't hurt to send up an offering to Menabozho or one of them other Chippewa spirits.''

Jim grinned. ''Kitshi Manitou,'' he said. ''He's more powerful.''

They all laughed.

Robbie and Jim had a second helping of sausages and eggs. Jim was in fine spirits. He talked of the old tribal gods and legends, of the Pukwudjinnies, little elves that the Indians believed inhabited the forest, and the Chippewa sandman, Weenk, who rode on the back of a firefly and put little children fast asleep. Instead of months, he said, the Indians had had moons. October was the harvest moon, and November was the moon of Menabozho, and December was the moon of the dripping horns.

''They meant antlers,'' Jim explained. ''That's when the deer shed their antlers.''

The wind howled through the eaves, but the kitchen was cozy and warm from the stove. Robbie began to feel better about things. It was lovely, he thought, what good food and good friends could do for your disposition.

15

From the south, the Soo Line tracks curved out of the woods below Palmatier's lumberyard, then ran straight to the depot. The depot was one of Robbie's favorite places. You could get away from things at the depot. When he was younger, he had gone up there nearly every day, he and Jim, climbing the wooden water tank and helping with the big iron-wheeled baggage carts and, on muggy days, horsing around Fancher's icehouse across the tracks.

Aunt Lib came up on Thursday. Robbie and his mother drove to the depot to meet her in Gramps' old '34 Studebaker. The wind gusted up the tracks and rattled the lid on the little coal-bin outside the waiting room. Mr.

Barnes, the stationmaster, saw them coming up the platform and rapped on the sliding window in the telegraph bay.

" 'Mornin', Madelyn!'' he called out, opening the window. " 'Mornin', Robbie! Waitin' on the *Limited?*''

"That's right, Jake,'' Madelyn VanEpp called back, holding her hat against the wind. "Is she on time?''

"Right on the button. Takes more'n a little blow to slow down the *Limited.*''

Mr. Barnes came around to hold the door for them. He wore a green eyeshade and had garters on his sleeves. Robbie liked the way men were quick to hold doors for his mother.

"Seems everybody's comin' and goin' these days, Madelyn,'' Mr. Barnes said, shutting the door behind them. "You expectin' Nate?''

"Not till next week, Jake,'' Madelyn VanEpp replied. "Libby's coming up for a few days. She was Wilma's maid of honor, you know.''

"My, that's nice of her,'' Mr. Barnes said. "Pity 'bout Wilma.''

The depot was warm and quiet except for the clattering of the telegraph. A fire was burning in the potbellied stove.

"My oldest boy left for National Guard camp yesterday,'' Mr. Barnes said.

"Buddy?'' Madelyn VanEpp said, surprised. "But he's just a boy!''

"Time flies, Madelyn,'' Mr. Barnes said. "We're none of us gettin' any younger.''

86

The *Limited* rumbled into the station, braking hard and streaked with the grime of the night.

"She's runnin' three minutes early!" Jake Barnes hollered over the noise.

The train seemed a special world to Robbie as the cars flashed by, first the day coaches, then the diner, then the sleepers with their elegant appointments and alluring names: "Chequamegon," "Governor Dodge," "Kettle Moraine."

"There's Mr. Reitmeyer!" Robbie called to his mother, and waved to the old conductor who had been just a brakeman when Gramps had been conductor of the *Limited*.

Everybody waved when the *Limited* pulled in. The people waved to the trainmen, and the trainmen waved to the people and to each other. Robbie waved back and looked for Aunt Lib. For a second he thought something had happened and she wasn't aboard. And then he spotted her, smiling and waving and the window all steamed up where her face pressed against it.

"Maddie, you look peaked," Aunt Lib said as the porter helped her down to the platform. "Robbie, you're growin' like a beanstalk."

Robbie lugged Aunt Lib's big leather-strapped suitcase to the car.

"How is Nate?" Madelyn VanEpp asked her sister.

"Oh, just fine, Maddie," Aunt Lib said, "except he's coming down with the hives from the change of water."

"Did he have any luck at Inland Tool?"

Aunt Lib shook her head. "That poor man!" she said.

"They've been slamming doors in his face left and right. He's going to apply at a few more places and then come home next Friday."

Robbie felt relieved.

"The Buhls are havin' their potluck Saturday, Aunt Lib," he said.

"Oh, I think I'll pass it by, Robbie," Aunt Lib said. "Your mother and I have some things to talk over. Besides, I want to spend some time with Wilma." She turned to her sister. "How is the poor thing?"

"It doesn't look good," Madelyn VanEpp said.

"It's a shame!" Aunt Lib said. "And in the prime of life! I brought her a box of Fanny May candy."

Robbie was always struck by the contrasts between his mother and Aunt Lib. Madelyn VanEpp was pretty and girlish and blushed when people told her how young she looked. Aunt Lib was stout and matronly, as if she had never been young, with heavy legs and a drooping chest and a nervous habit of sniffing her fingers.

"The McIntosh are coming in, Libby," Madelyn VanEpp said. "We could put up some applesauce for you to take back."

Madelyn VanEpp spent the rest of the day in the kitchen while Aunt Lib visited with Mrs. Houtekier. After supper, Robbie started a fire in the fireplace. They pulled a table up close to it and played rummy. It was very nice, Robbie thought, the warmth of the fire and the wind howling outside. He was glad there had been no difficulties. There were usually difficulties when Aunt Lib visited.

But late that night he woke up in a sweat. He sensed something was wrong. He looked out the window. The scudding clouds shut out the moon, and the wind rattled the shutters. He heard the icebox door slam downstairs, and then voices, loud, angry voices.

"No! Next year will be too late. Myron needs that money now, Maddie. It's a chance to put us on Easy Street."

"But move to Chicago without Nate even having a job? Libby, it's insane."

"No, it's not. With your share of the house money you could make out fine till Nate lined something up."

"But, Libby — "

"This is my house as much as it is yours, Maddie. Baba wanted us to share and share alike, and so did Gramps. It was only out of the goodness of our hearts that Myron and I didn't press you to sell sooner."

"Good Lord, Libby! What did you expect us to do, go on relief?"

"I don't care, Maddie. Myron has worked hard all his life. He's entitled to a chance."

"No, Libby. I won't do it. At least not right now. It would break Robbie's heart. You can at least wait till he finishes at Holy Childhood."

"That little crackerbox of a school? Maddie, you could enroll him at one of the good public schools, Austin, maybe, or Carl Schurz, and then he could apply for a scholarship at Loyola. It's not right for a boy of his ability to be cooped up in Sister Bay, traipsing around with that Indian and Charlie and that big galoot of a Swede . . ."

Robbie buried his head in the pillows to shut out the arguing. It upset him to hear grownups yelling at each other. *Think on things of good report,* Sister Joan Therese had always told him. *Shut out a bad thought with a good thought.*

Robbie thought of Loon Lodge. It would be different with them. They would never say mean things or do mean things. He pictured how it would be in the mornings, waking up to the happy smells of bacon frying and coffee perking and pine logs crackling in the fireplace. They would make buttermilk pancakes, and laugh and joke and talk of their possibilities.

He fell asleep praying: *Dear God and the Virgin Mary and all the saints, please help us to get the land on the Up Holly. The land will make us safe. We will fence it in, and things will always stay the same . . .*

16

The next day the blow settled into a cold, driving rain. The skies were gray and heavy, and the rain swept across the bay in rippling sheets.

Robbie spent the morning washing storm windows out in the garage, and then in the afternoon he put on his slicker to run errands for Mr. Houtekier, at Arbuckle's and the post office and Burr's hardware. The rain stung his face as he walked into it.

"Today should be the end of it," Mr. Burr said. Mr. Houtekier's order was already wrapped, a little brown package that rattled when Robbie shook it. "She'll start windin' down tomorrow."

"It's been a fine blow, hasn't it, Mr. Burr?" Robbie said.

"Oh my, yes, Robbie," Mr. Burr agreed. "It's been one of the best. Well, say hello to your ma."

As Robbie came up Arcadian, he saw young Doc Davies leaving the Houtekiers'.

"What did he say?" Robbie asked Mr. Houtekier. "I mean, is there any chance of her gettin' better?"

" 'Tain't likely, Robbie," Odie Houtekier said. He looked tired and worried, and his mind seemed to wander. "Would you mind sittin' with Wilma for a bit, Robbie? I've got some business to tend to at the co-op."

"Yes, sir," Robbie said.

Robbie was startled to see how rapidly Wilma Houtekier was wasting away. It seemed each day there was a little less of her, as if she were evaporating and there were no stopping it. This afternoon, however, there was a touch of color in her pale cheeks.

"Rouge," she said, with an apologetic little smile. "Seems a woman's vanity stays with her to the end."

Robbie came around the bed and fluffed up the pillows. An old photograph album and a magnifying glass lay in Mrs. Houtekier's lap.

"Shoot, you'll be up 'n around in no time."

"You needn't play games with me, Robbie VanEpp." She pulled her knitted blue bedjacket around her. "There's no helpin' what I've got. I've resigned myself."

Robbie got out the checkerboard and pulled a rocker up to the bed.

92

"Red or black?" he asked.

"Red, I think, Robbie," Mrs. Houtekier said. "I'm in a red mood today." She pointed to the vase on the commode. "Your chrysanthemums are lovely."

"I pinched them back in July just like you said. It was the pinching back that did it."

Robbie arranged the checkers on the board. The wind rattled the windowpanes and blew the petals from the morning-glories that grew on strings up the side of the house.

"Your Aunt Lib says you folks'll be movin' to Chicago for sure."

"That's a lot of bull," Robbie said. "Uncle Myron's got another business scheme cooked up, and they want their share of the house."

"A fallin' out over money?"

Robbie grinned. "I guess so," he said.

"It isn't really the money, Robbie," Mrs. Houtekier said. "It's resentment. When you reach middle age, it seems all the slights and petty grievances of your childhood come festerin' out. Money's just an excuse."

She made a deep sigh.

"We're children under the skin, Robbie, all the way to the grave. You can have fame and riches and do great things, but in the end your childhood is all that matters. Remember that, Robbie, when you have children of your own. Give them good memories."

"Yes, ma'am," Robbie said.

They played three games of checkers. Robbie thumbed

through the album as they played. There was a picture of Alvia Ivors wearing a fur hat and muff and posing in front of a snowman in Silurian Park, and another one of a group of people on the lawn at Moonrise.

"That was at one of the outings the Senator held every summer for folks around the lake," Mrs. Houtekier said. "That's Hubert Locke next to Alvia, the one with all the medals."

"He got shot down, didn't he?"

"Yes, but the Senator chased him off long before that. The Senator chased off all her beaus. And over here, in the bathing suit, recognize her?"

"No."

"Lela Buhl."

"Really?" Robbie said, and laughed.

"Oh, Lela was quite a belle in her day."

"What's that thing going into the ground down on the beach?" Robbie asked. "Looks like a cave."

"Oh, the Senator got tired of folks traipsin' through the house in wet bathing suits, and so he put in a tunnel that ran down to the landing. But there was a cave-in and he had it filled in."

"What was Alvia like when she was a girl?"

"Like you," Wilma Houtekier said. "A regular tomboy, fishin' the Narrows and trampin' through the woods and forever taggin' after Billy Sashabaw. But when she blossomed, lands, those were the days! The guests would come in on the *Limited,* and the carriages would be lined

94

up at the depot with those fine Morgan horses all shiny and groomed.''

"How come the Senator ran off Alvia's beaus?''

"Oh, he wasn't a happy man, Robbie,'' Wilma Houtekier said. "His wife dyin' in childbirth even before Moonrise was completed, and then Junior and his wife suffocatin' in that fire. They said Junior had been drinkin' and was careless with a cigar. Little Alvia was asleep in her crib in the next room. Lands, Billy Sashabaw got to her in the nick of time!''

"Billy Sashabaw?'' Robbie said. "But I thought it was the Senator that rescued her.''

"The Senator let everybody think that,'' Mrs. Houtekier said, "but it was really Billy Sashabaw. Maybe that was why the Senator came to resent him so much.''

"Whatever happened to Billy?''

"Nobody knows, Robbie. He sort of came and went on his own terms. One day he just hopped the northbound *Limited* and never came back. There was talk of some kind of fallin' out between him and the Senator — ''

Wilma Houtekier appeared to be tiring.

"I guess I wore you out with all my questions,'' Robbie apologized.

"No, Robbie.'' She sighed and let the album fall shut. "It's a joy to remember it.'' She looked out the window at the morning-glories. "They'll be gone soon. They're stubborn flowers, but they'll be gone like everything else.''

And then she made a little gasp and sat up straight in the bed.

"Is the pain startin' up again?" Robbie asked.

"Yes, Robbie." Wilma Houtekier's face had become drawn and there was a tenseness in her body. "You'd best run on home."

"Is there anything I can do?"

"No, Robbie. Pain can't be shared. Just run along home. Tell your Aunt Lib I'll be resting tonight, but that she can come over in the morning if she'd like."

Robbie put the checkerboard away and slipped into his slicker. He felt guilty about leaving. He wished he could take some of the pain from Mrs. Houtekier and put it in his own body. It didn't seem fair for her to have it all.

"Have you been lookin' after Charlie, Robbie?" Wilma Houtekier asked.

"Yes, ma'am. We've been tryin' to."

"Good. And look after Sister Bay. Look after your town."

"Yes, ma'am."

At the door, Robbie stopped and turned.

"Mrs. Houtekier?"

"Yes, Robbie?"

"Is dyin' hard?"

The rain tapped on the windowpanes.

"No, Robbie," Wilma Houtekier said, quietly. "The pain is hard, but the dying isn't. Things are straight in my mind, you see. That's why it isn't hard."

Robbie left the house and walked in the dusk in the rain.

17

Since dawn the heavy odors of cooking had come from the kitchen at Buhl Farm. Now Lela Buhl took the last crock of beans from the oven and set it on the sideboard to cool.

"Lands!" she sighed, sinking into a chair for a minute to let the rushing sensation clear from her head. "Makes a body feel her age!"

It was done, finally, the bread baked, the buffet tables all nicely arranged on the lawn, the lanterns strung in the trees. The beer tent would be around by the icehouse this year, and if the men wanted anything stronger they could just have it in the parking area Henry had roped off in the pasture. The Swede was bringing his Victrola, and Heinie and the band had promised to be there early. Still it would be nice to roll the piano out on the porch; Millie Horton might want to play.

"Robbie 'n Jim can do it when we get back from the Up Holly, Ma," Livvie Buhl said, cutting the last of the carrot sticks at the sink.

"I wish you weren't traipsin' off to the Up Holly today of all days, Livvie," Lela Buhl said.

"But Jim's takin' the train up to the reservation tonight, Ma," Livvie said. "It'll be our last chance to put up the sign. Now you just sit there and rest for a bit. What fun's a party if the hostess can't enjoy herself?"

It was always the best affair on the lake, the Buhls' annual potluck. Lela Buhl had a way with things; everybody said so. And coming as it did in September, with the summer people gone and the harvest well underway, it was more relaxing than the Arbuckles' or the VanEpps' or the Houtekiers' potlucks, although Wilma Houtekier had quite a flair herself.

"Livvie," Lela Buhl said, "don't let me forget to send a plate down to Odie and Wilma."

"Shorty said she can't take solids, Ma."

"Makes no never-mind, dear," Lela Buhl said. "You send whether a body eats it or not."

"Can I fix a plate for the Swede to take up to Charlie, Ma?" Livvie asked.

" 'Course you can, dear," Lela Buhl said. "And put in a slice of your cherry pie. Charlie likes your cherry pie."

98

Livvie went to the window where the pies were cooling. It was perfect weather for an outing. The blow had left everything cool and clean and clear. Across the lake, at Moonrise, a silver flagpole showed above the trees, but there was no flag.

"The Herr Doktor isn't flyin' the state flag," Livvie said. "Alvia Ivors always flew the state flag."

Lela Buhl went to the window to see. The state flag had been one of the Senator's traditions. You should always fly the state flag, he had said, even without the national flag, for the states were the nation.

"I reckon you'll be seein' a lot of changes over there," she said, "with the Herr Doktor runnin' the show."

"How come he took over so soon, Ma?" Livvie asked.

"The estate was in debt, Livvie," her mother replied. "Alvia's will specified everything was to be sold to satisfy the creditors. The Herr Doktor was holdin' most of the paper."

Livvie poured her mother a cup of coffee from the stove, and they both sat down at the table.

"I just don't understand it," Livvie said. "The Senator was supposed to have been such a fine man, how'd he ever get mixed up with the Herr Doktor?"

"Oh, it was at one of them German spas or whatever," Lela Buhl said, "when he 'n Alvia was makin' the grand tour. They were hardly off the boat when he came down with one of his asthma attacks. The Herr Doktor had a remedy the Senator swore by, so he brought him over here and gave him that land over on the cove so's he'd be close by. Pity. Only foolish thing Arthur Ivors ever did, but who was to know?''

She stirred her coffee and rambled on.

''From the start he was always sort of uppity, the Herr Doktor. Not once has he set foot in a house socially. Not once! 'Course nobody's ever invited him over that I can recall. He just didn't — well, he didn't seem to fit in, don'tcha know? Still, it might of been different if he hadn't sent Gerta Brandt packin' — ''

''Gerta Brandt?'' Livvie said.

''She was his nurse, Livvie. She was there that time Robbie split his head open at the powwow, remember? That was when the Herr Doktor was still tendin' to his medicine instead of actin' like a tycoon. Gerta was the best thing that ever happened to him, but the grass always looks greener, and he was chasin' after some slip of a schoolteacher up in Hayward.''

''How come Alvia never married, Ma?'' Livvie said. ''Everybody says she was the belle of the lake.''

''Lands!'' Lela Buhl exclaimed. ''What's all this pryin' about folks that is dead?''

Livvie cupped her chin in her hands.

''I don't know, Ma,'' she said. ''It's just I've got a feelin' there was somethin' tragic about Alvia, somethin' mysterious.''

''Pshaw!'' Lela Buhl scoffed. ''Robbie 'n Jim have been fillin' your head with notions. You should be seein' more of Muriel Pease and Loretta Runstrom, Livvie.

100

When a girl's your age, she should be thinkin' of ladylike things.''

"What for, Ma? I already know what I'm goin' to do with my life.''

"Robbie VanEpp, I suppose, and Loon Lodge?''

"Uh-huh," Livvie replied.

Lela Buhl sighed. "Things change, Livvie. Loon Lodge is a fine dream, but a lot could happen 'fore you 'n Robbie come of age. And what if they send Charlie to jail? Who'll apply for the homestead then?''

"Pa could do it.''

"Your pa's set in his ways, Livvie. He believes people should earn what they get out of life.''

"I know, Ma," Livvie said. "Robbie wouldn't ask anyway. He thinks it's wrong to ask for things.''

"Well, what if somebody buys that land 'fore you get a chance at it?''

"But Robbie's determined, Ma.''

"Sometimes determination ain't enough, Livvie. Sometimes life's a settling for second-best. You ought not to leave yourself so exposed. What if Robbie meets another girl?''

Livvie laughed. "Oh, Ma! You're a regular wet blanket.''

"But a girl's got to be sure of things, Livvie," Lela Buhl said. "Marriage is a commitment, a no-nonsense commitment to stick by a person no matter what. A lot of folks never make the commitment and spend the rest of

101

their lives eatin' their hearts out over might-have-beens. Have you made that kind of commitment, Livvie?''

"Shoot, Ma, ever since that time Robbie came to see me in the hospital, I guess.''

"And Robbie? Has Robbie made the commitment?''

Livvie looked out the window, a trace of uncertainty showing in her eyes. "I'm not sure, Ma,'' she said, softly. "Sometimes I think so, but I'm not sure.''

"You'd best be sure, Livvie,'' Lela Buhl said. "You'd best be sure as shootin'. Life's hard, Livvie. There'll be sorrow and pain and hardship, but there'll be good things too, joy and laughter and the good times around the table. And if you've both made the commitment the good will outweigh the bad, and then when you look back you wouldn't trade a minute of it. But you've got to be sure, Livvie. It's a terrible thing to burst with love and never know for sure whether what you feel in your heart is returned.''

Livvie Buhl slipped into her mother's lap and hugged her tight.

"Don't worry, Ma,'' she said. "Robbie'll make the commitment. You'll see. When the time comes, I'll be a belle just like Alvia Ivors, and Robbie'll come sing under my window, strummin' his ukulele and just moonsick with love — ''

She began to sing, her voice high and clear.

"Ohhh, Buffalo Gal, won't you come out tonight,
Come out tonight, come out tonight — ''

"Come on, Ma!" Livvie urged. "Sing! It'll do your spirits good!"

"Livvie!" Lela Buhl blushed. "I've got things to do!"

But she sang, and their voices carried out the window and up to the barn, where Henry Buhl paused in his chores and smiled.

"Buffalo Gal, won't you come out tonight,
And dance by the light of the moon?"

18

The Swede had often said Up Holly Bay reminded him of Gotland where he had lived as a boy. The shale bluffs rose fifty feet in places, sheltering the bay from the strong north winds and giving it a cavernous quality as with a fiord. Thick green vines grew straight down to the water, and tall pines lined the precipices above.

Robbie curved the *Ruby Allen* into the bay wide open and moving with the wind. It felt good, he thought, the way the boat leaned into the turn.

"Slow down!" Jim hollered from the bow. "You'll run us out of gas!" He grinned and Robbie grinned back. It was a fine day to be out on the lake.

Robbie cut the motor and let the *Ruby Allen* coast in

toward shore. Jim broke out the oars while Livvie scrambled back and helped Robbie secure the Evinrude. Gasoline trickled down and made little rainbows on the water. The lake was choppy but the bay was smooth, and the air had a clean pine scent to it.

"Careful of the loon nests, Jim," Livvie said.

Jim worked the oars and kept them pointed toward a clump of trees at a spot where the bluffs dropped abruptly to the shoreline. They ducked down to avoid the branches. The trees concealed an oval-shaped inlet, deep with tiny white pebbles showing on the bottom. The banks jutted up like walls, solid gray shale streaked with moss.

"We'll have the best landing on the whole lake," Livvie said.

"It's a swell spot all right," Robbie said. "Next summer we'll sink the pilings for the pier."

They crawled out at a spot where the shale rose from the water in little terraces.

"You follow behind Jim, Livvie," Robbie said. "I'll carry the sign."

Jim led the way up the path they had already beaten down in the woods. The path was soft and cool and matted with pine needles. The woods ran across the face of a hill, then opened on a wide sloping meadow. There was a wonderful view, from the hills of Court Oreilles to the north all the way down to the Narrows. Across the lake, in the distance, Thunder Ridge rose like a rumble of green against the pale blue sky.

105

"Maybe we could have a flagpole," Livvie said. "We could fly the state flag if we had a flagpole."

"Yeah," Robbie said. "A flagpole would be swell."

"That could be one of Charlie's jobs," Jim said, "raisin' the flag every day."

"Golly, I forgot," Livvie said. "What about a place for Charlie to wave at the cars?"

"Maybe with a place of his own," Robbie said, "Charlie won't want to wave at the cars."

In the center of the meadow stood an immense white oak, like a gnarled sentry, its branches so thick and heavy they hung down close to the ground. Some names had been carved in the trunk.

TOM LENROOT
RED WEIRGOR
1876

Robbie and Livvie held the sign while Jim nailed it to the tree with two old railroad spikes. It was a large, thick rectangle of oak stained to a deep brown and finished with several coats of shellac.

LOON LODGE
1939

"I feel better havin' the sign up," Jim said. "It'll give us somethin' to shoot for."

"How long you think it'll take us, Jim?" Livvie said.

106

"Loon Lodge ain't somethin' you finish, Livvie," Jim said. "You keep workin' at it forever."

They started up the hill. A fringe of hemlocks grew above the meadow, and above the hemlocks a thick stand of white birches. The birches gave everything a clean, airy feeling. The hill flattened out on the crest, then sloped away to the east.

"We'll build the house up here," Robbie said, "way back in the birches."

"We'll need some kind of plans," Jim said.

"I'll draw them," Livvie said. "I helped Pa when he built the new barn."

They walked back down to the meadow and stretched out in the grass. They would clear the bottomland east of the hill first, Robbie said, using the logs for the pier and a temporary cabin. An access road would come next, and then would begin the backbreaking job of clearing additional acreage for cultivation. The meadow would do for a pasture just as it was, he said, at least for the time being.

"Pa says farming'll break your heart at times," Livvie said, "but that it's proper work for a person."

"Oh, it'll be hard at first," Jim said, "but we'll make do. We'll buy flour and salt and stuff at Arbuckle's, but mostly we'll live off the land."

A flock of loons swooped down over the birches and went out of sight over the bay.

" 'Course havin' the lodge don't mean we'll live here all the time," Robbie said. "We'll do a lot of travelin', maybe go round the world, even."

"Travelin'?" Livvie said, perplexed. "But what for, Robbie?"

"Shoot, Livvie," Robbie said, "a person's got to do things, see things. But we'll always come back to Sister Bay on account of this is where we belong."

"But who'd look after Charlie?" Livvie said. "We couldn't go gallivantin' around and leave Charlie here by himself."

"She's right, Robbie," Jim said. "He could have a spell and die."

"And what if they send Charlie to Mendota?" Livvie went on. "What then?"

"Don't worry, Livvie," Jim said. "Nobody's goin' to send Charlie to Mendota."

"But supposin' they do, Jim," Livvie said. "Will he still be a partner?"

"Shoot, Livvie," Jim said, "Loon Lodge was Charlie's idea in the first place. You can't run out on your partners."

"Even if Charlie gets sick and can't do his fair share?"

Jim nodded. "Even then."

Livvie made a little smile. "Oh, I'm so glad," she sighed. "It was beginning to seem we cared more about the homestead application than we did about Charlie."

They spent the remainder of the afternoon beating down a path to the eastern boundary of the acreage. A mist was forming on the meadow when they finally started down to the *Ruby Allen*. An orange-and-purple glow spread slowly over the horizon as the last tip of the sun disappeared behind Thunder Ridge. There was the special stillness that comes at dusk. Across the lake, the sounds of merry-making echoed out from Buhl farm.

"Roll out the barrel,
We've got the blues on the run — "

"Whereabouts you figure the sun is now, Jim?" Livvie said. "Over Minnesota?"

"Farther'n that, Livvie," Jim said. "Montana, maybe."

"Isn't it lovely," Livvie said, "how everybody in the whole world gets to see the same sun?"

At the bottom of the meadow they stopped and looked back up at the sign. The cry of a loon pierced the still-ness. A little thrill ran through Livvie. The cry of the loon was spooky in a way but exciting and truly wild. Suddenly she started jumping up and down and dancing around.

"Oh, I feel I could burst!" she cried. "It's goin' to be a swell farm, isn't it? It's goin' to be the swellest farm in the whole world!"

She threw her slender arms around Robbie and twirled through the air.

"Can I be a blood brother now, Robbie?" she said. "Can I, please?"

They stood in a circle while Jim took his knife and

pricked their fingers. They smeared the blood in the palm of Jim's hand. Then Jim kicked up some loose earth and rubbed his hand in it.

"That way," he said, "our blood'll be part of Loon Lodge forever."

A blue heron was coming in over the Up Holly.

19

Everybody said it was the nicest potluck they could
remember. The ladies had all brought their special dishes,
casseroles and relishes and golden pies with latticed crusts.
There were steins of Old Style Lager and mugs of apple
cider, and on the spit behind the barn one of Henry Buhl's
prize porkers was sizzling to a crispy brown. The air was
filled with music and good smells, and, for a while at
least, families from up and down the lake sang and danced
and forgot their cares.

Lela Buhl seemed to be everywhere at once, urging the
guests to sample a bit of this or a bit of that, and there was
much oohing and aahing and exchanging of recipes.

"Seems every year there's a few more faces missin',

Lela," remarked Herman Rosenfelder, who looked ill-at-ease in a starched collar. " 'Tain't right, city folks runnin' up here and livin' high on the hog and local folks traipsin' to the cities for fancy jobs in defense plants."

"The grass always looks greener, Herman," Lela Buhl said, shaking her head sadly. "Some day they'll come runnin' back. Mark my words!"

A platform for dancing had been set up under the trees, and over near the hedgerow the farm ladies crowded around a gaily decorated booth to have their palms read by "Gypsy Donna Bella," who was really Millie Horton in an exotic costume with earrings and a veil.

"The Swede's been lookin' for you," Millie called to Robbie as he and Livvie and Jim came up from the landing.

"Is he beered up, Millie?" Robbie asked.

"Not yet," Millie laughed, "but he's workin' on it."

Livvie let Millie read her palm.

"I see a tall dark man comin' into your life," Millie said, tracing a finger over the lines in Livvie's palm.

Livvie giggled and blushed. Jim grinned and poked Robbie. "Guess that lets you out, Robbie," he said, "less'n you dye your hair black."

Robbie laughed and pulled Jim's hat down over his eyes, and for a minute the two of them roughhoused about, jabbing at each other with little rabbit punches.

"Millie says she thinks the Swede's goin' to propose soon," Livvie said, as they moved away from the booth.

"The Swede get married?" Robbie scoffed. "Shoot, he's got a good life the way it is."

"Oh, I don't know," Livvie said. "It's lonely when you're all by yourself."

The Swede, in his Sunday best and wearing a straw hat, was up in the beer tent arguing politics with Shorty Arbuckle.

"Chamberlain oughta just give 'em the whole shebang, if you ask me," Shorty was saying. He was a tall skinny man with a goiter. "Est*on*ia and *Lat*via and Lith*awhat*chamacallit. Not a one of 'em as big as Sawyer County, and forever at each other's throats!"

"You'll sing a different tune, Shorty," the Swede said, "when Adolph Hitler comes sailin' up the Fox River."

"The Fox River?" Shorty said, and laughed. "Why, you're a regular riot, Swede."

The Swede took Robbie around to the icehouse to help him roll out another keg of beer.

"Don't forget, we're seein' Stanfill P. Stanfill tomorrow," the Swede said. "Three o'clock, Dew Drop Inn."

"How does it look, Swede?"

"I don't know, Robbie. You figured out where that music box might be?"

Robbie shook his head.

"Then I guess it don't look so good."

The Swede brushed the sawdust from the keg and sat down on it for a minute.

"We-ll, Robbie — " he said, "I guess all you can do is

tell Stan what you saw over at Billy Sashabaw's lake. Maybe he'll do a little pokin' round on his own."

"Yeah," Robbie said. "Maybe."

"Did you kids make out that deposition like Stan asked?"

"Yeah," Robbie said, "but a fat lot of good that's goin' to do."

"It ain't as hopeless as it seems, Robbie," the Swede said. "Stanfill P. Stanfill says it's the job of the district attorney to keep folks from bein' picked on. He'll look after Charlie."

When it got dark, Henry Buhl lit the Japanese lanterns that were strung in the trees. The lanterns flickered in the breeze and gave off a happy glow. Jim went back to take his turn at the spit, and Livvie went in to fix a plate for Robbie to take down to Wilma Houtekier. Robbie started over to get another mug of cider and then noticed a little commotion around the dance floor.

"She's dancing! She's dancing!"

Robbie ran down to see. There was the trill of the accordion and the oom-pah-pah of the tuba, and then Lela Buhl and Herman Rosenfelder were out on the floor by themselves doing a polka. Herman Rosenfelder was clowning around and trying to balance a stein of beer on his head, but every eye was on Lela Buhl, her shoulders held back, her elbows thrust out, and her heavy legs kicking high. Everybody gathered round and hooted and clapped.

"Atta girl, Lela!"

114

"Show 'em how, Lela!"

"A-a-ah, ha-a-a!"

And as the dancers flew about the floor, an oddly wistful mood seemed to come over the weatherbeaten farmers and their wives. Robbie sensed that somehow it was a very special moment, as if the sight of Lela Buhl kicking up her heels made the years fall away.

There was a big round of applause as Lela Buhl collapsed onto a bench.

"Lands!" she gasped, fanning herself with her apron. "Haven't done so much dancin' since Henry 'n I was courtin'."

The music and laughter echoed out over the lake till well into the night. Lela Buhl was relieved there had been no incidents. But, later, when the Swede and Herman Rosenfelder got into an Indian-wrestling contest down on the pier and both of them toppled into the drink, she decided they'd had enough.

"Jim," she ordered, "hop in the *Mary Ann* and run Herman home. You'll have plenty of time to catch your train. Robbie, you 'n Livvie collect the Swede's Victrola and run him home in the *Ruby Allen*."

The Swede looked a mess, his tie askew and his wet double-breasted suit shrinking up around his wrists. *"In the Big Rock Candy Mountains,"* he crooned, heaving his stein out into the lake, *"you never change your socks —"*

"Hush, Swede!" Lela Buhl laughed. "You'll have the Herr Doktor over here with the deputy."

Millie Horton, still in her gypsy costume, ran down to the pier and tugged at the Swede's arm.

"But they're playin' our polka, Swede!" she coaxed. "You promised!"

The Swede leaned over and whispered something in Millie's ear. Millie giggled and blushed, then turned and ran up to the house.

"Home, Jeeves!" Herman Rosenfelder said to Jim, and climbed into the *Mary Ann*.

Jim turned to Robbie and Livvie.

"Well," he said, "I guess this is it."

"Goodbye, my Chippewa boy," Livvie said. She gave Jim a big hug and a kiss. "Take good care of yourself."

Jim grinned shyly, then gave Robbie their special handshake.

"So long, Robbie," he said. "Take it slow."

For an instant, Robbie felt tears welling up in his eyes. Summer was finally over, completely and irrevocably over, and now his friend was going back to Court Oreilles to his people.

"You take it slow too, Jim," he replied. "Don't forget, two long and three short for the Flambeau."

Then Herman Rosenfelder stood up unsteadily in the *Mary Ann* and faced Lela Buhl. He was a comical figure in a way, short and rotund with a red face and flowing white hair, but now there was a great dignity about him.

"My compliments, Lela," he said, bowing low and making a little flourish with his soggy straw hat. "Another sweet memory to comfort me in the winter of life — "

116

And then they were gone, Herman Rosenfelder and Jim and the *Mary Ann,* and as Lela Buhl turned and hurried up the hedgerow, tears began streaming down her tired face. Livvie ran after her mother and took her hand.

"What is it, Ma?" she said, a worried look on her face.

Lela Buhl laughed in embarrassment.

"Lands!" she said, fumbling for a handkerchief. "Don't know what's come over your old ma. Nerves, I suppose." She wiped her eyes and blew her nose. "That Herman Rosenfelder! Makes a body feel it's the end of the world. Now you 'n Robbie scoot 'fore the Swede decides to pay another visit to the beer tent."

The night was very still and the lake was very calm. Every now and then a fish leaped out of the water, leaving little ripples on the surface. The ripples glittered in the moonlight. Robbie decided to row up to the Swede's. The sounds of the night were friendly guideposts, and the outboard would shut them out.

The Swede was still singing.

> *"Railroad Bill, goin' down the hill,*
> *Lightin' cigars with a five dollar bill —"*

Robbie tried to keep cadence with the oars, but the Swede kept singing faster and faster till Robbie was thrashing about so wildly that the *Ruby Allen* started going around in circles. The three of them flopped back in their seats, laughing so hard they couldn't catch their breath.

Robbie looked up at the sky. It seemed every star in the

universe was out. He looked for Cassiopeia, found it, and then the Big Dipper. It was as if it were all one great consciousness, the stars and the sky and the earth below it, and that somehow he was a part of it.

"Oh, it's been such a lovely day!" Livvie sighed. "It's almost like bein' in heaven."

"But this is heaven, Livvie," the Swede said.

Livvie giggled. "Oh, go on, Swede!"

"I mean it, Livvie. This is all you get, so enjoy it while you can."

Livvie let her hand trail in the water.

"But what about the Bible, Swede?" she said, softly.

"Oh-hh, I don't know," the Swede said. "The cherubim and seraphim never struck me as bein' reasonable. But it really don't matter. You've got to live life well for its own sake, Livvie. You've got to live it clean and pure so that there'll be no regrets. The worst thing in the world is for a man to look back and wonder what it was all for anyway."

Robbie took the oars and rowed quietly up the lake. The sound of crickets came out from the shore. He had never particularly looked forward to the heaven of the Bible. It seemed pious and stern and no fun. He had imagined a different kind of heaven, a heaven of first snowfalls and Indian summers and soft spring evenings. Gramps and Baba and everybody would be there, and they would relive all the good times.

"Well, if Sister Bay is heaven," Livvie said after a while, "then what's hell?"

The Swede scooped up a handful of water and splashed it on his face.

"I don't know, Livvie," he said. "Maybe hell is knowin' it won't last."

As Robbie veered the *Ruby Allen* in toward the Swede's place, he noticed a slender figure come out of the woods and hurry up to the house. It was Millie Horton.

Robbie and Livvie said good night to the Swede, then started through the woods. The moonlight made silver patterns on the path that wound along the lake down to Buhl Farm.

"He's got Millie in there," Livvie said, "hasn't he?"

"How'd you know?" Robbie said.

"I could tell," Livvie said. "Women can always tell."

They fell into silence. From deep in the woods came the melancholy call of a whippoorwill. Livvie sensed that all the talk about heaven and death had upset Robbie.

"Just because the Swede says so, Robbie," she said, "doesn't mean it's so."

"I don't know, Livvie. The Swede's pretty smart."

"Then after you died," Livvie said, "there'd be nothing."

"I guess so."

"I can't imagine nothing."

"No," Robbie said, "neither can I."

Robbie sensed something was wrong the minute they came out of the woods and headed up toward the farmhouse. The music had stopped and the guests were leaving. They could make out Henry Buhl directing the last of the pickups out of the pasture, dust clouding up in the beams of the headlights.

"Something must've happened," Livvie said.

"Maybe war's been declared," Robbie said.

Lela Buhl saw the youngsters coming across the alfalfa meadow and hurried down to meet them.

"Livvie, you run on up to your room," she said, her face pale and drawn in the moonlight. "Robbie, Mr. Buhl's waitin' on you."

"What is it, Ma?" Livvie said.

"There's been some trouble," Lela Buhl replied. "Odie Houtekier killed Wilma. Just blew her brains right out. Said he couldn't stand to see her suffer no more."

A cool wind was beginning to blow up off the lake. A little chill went through Robbie. He hadn't noticed it before but his feet were cold from the mist on the meadow. He wondered who would look after Mrs. Houtekier's clematis vines. Surely they would wither and die without her.

"Stanfill P. Stanfill's on his way down from Hayward," Lela Buhl said. "Hurry along now. It's going to be a long night for us."

20

The moon was up high by the time Henry Buhl rounded the creamery and started to ease his old pickup down Bluff Road.

"Tell your ma Miz Buhl'll be down in the morning to help with things at the Houtekiers'," he said to Robbie.

"Yes, sir," Robbie said.

"I suppose they'll be lockin' Odie up. Pity."

Robbie watched the familiar landmarks slip by in the shadows — the hatchery, the co-op, Horace Ward's Red Crown station.

"It ain't like it's a regular murder, is it?" he said. "I mean, everybody knew Mrs. Houtekier was goin' to die anyway."

"No, Robbie, it ain't," Henry Buhl said. "For a fact it ain't."

"I picked up some shells for Mr. Houtekier yesterday."

"Some shells?"

"Unh-hunh. Up at Burr's."

"Twenty-twos?"

"Couldn't tell," Robbie said. "They were already wrapped. But they were shells all right. I shook the box."

They turned up Arcadian. Lights were still burning in most of the houses. The kerosene lamps gave off a friendly glow. Next year the Rural Electrification Administration would have everything electrified. Main Street was already hooked up, and there was an arc light in front of Lydia's Five & Dime. Robbie wondered what the town would look like with electric lights.

"Robbie?" Henry Buhl said.

"Yes, sir?"

"I wouldn't mention nothin' 'bout pickin' up them shells. No sense in settin' tongues to waggin' more'n they already are. Understand?"

"Yes, sir," Robbie said. "I understand."

Henry Buhl shook his head.

"Goes to show you, Robbie," he said. "Never make hasty judgments about a man. People're full of surprises. Yessir, full of 'em!"

Madelyn VanEpp sent Robbie straight to bed.

"Aunt Lib and I are going to wait up for Stanfill P. Stanfill," she said.

122

"Is Aunt Lib going to stay for the funeral?"

"No, she's too upset. She's leaving in the morning on the local. Besides, Wilma is being buried in Black River Falls. The family plot is down there."

Robbie undressed in the dark, then pulled a rocker up to the window and looked out over the cherry trees to the Houtekiers'. The shades were drawn in the downstairs room where Mrs. Houtekier had been confined since she became ill. Robbie wondered if they had pulled the sheets up over her. They always pulled the sheets over you. Maybe they had put handcuffs on Mr. Houtekier. The deputy would like that, putting handcuffs on somebody.

He leaned back in the rocker and stared up at the ceiling. It seemed unthinkable that such a tragedy could have occurred so close to his bedroom. His bedroom had always been safe and secure. There were two iron beds with patch quilts that his grandmother, Baba, had made. Next to each bed stood a commode with a kerosene lamp. There was another lamp on the wall next to the door, and a square of sandpaper for striking matches. The lamps made the shadows dance on the walls. In the middle of the floor was a metal grate that you could open on cool mornings to let the heat up from the kitchen — and the smells of coffee perking and bacon frying. It was nice getting up on cool mornings; it felt so good when you got warm.

"You get straight into bed, young man!" It was Madelyn VanEpp calling up from the kitchen. "No fooling around, you hear?"

"Okay, *okay!*" Robbie called back.

He slipped into bed and struggled to stay awake till Stanfill P. Stanfill arrived. It was difficult to stay awake after a day out on the lake. The lake cleaned you out, and sleep came quickly. The wind rustled in the trees and rattled the climber on the trellis below his window. He wished Gramps were there. It was hard not having Gramps around to explain things. Nate VanEpp wasn't an explaining kind of father. None of the fathers Robbie knew were, except maybe Mr. Buhl.

It was the violence that was disturbing, he thought. And yet it shouldn't be. There was violence everywhere. The forest was violent, the Narrows was violent, fishing was violent. *"The worms crawl in, the worms crawl out."* It must have been a bloodthirsty God who thought it all up. Robbie thought of how a chicken ran around after its head was chopped off, and then he thought of *A Tale of Two Cities* and how they put people to death in France. Maybe people ran around after their heads were chopped off. Maybe the head never died.

They had thought up so many ways of doing it. He had read that in Utah they strapped you in a chair and shot you. Down in Joliet they electrocuted you, in a little room with a green door, and the lights dimmed when the man threw the switch. It must be a terrible way to go, your flesh sizzling and your body jerking and the acrid smell. Hanging was probably best, although there must be an awful moment when your neck snapped.

But they didn't do any of those ugly things in Wiscon-

124

sin. Wisconsin was special. They would put Mr. Houtekier in Waupun, and he would wear convict stripes and rattle his spoon in the mess hall. Robbie wondered how he had done it — if they had agreed on it, if they had said an act of contrition, if he had got her from the front or sneaked up behind, if he had used the twenty-two or the twelve-gauge, if it had been messy.

Gramps had wet the bed the night he died. He just went to sleep and never woke up. Everybody said it was a swell way to go. Aunt Lib had given Robbie a flower from the grave, a zinnia, for his prayer book. Ever since, the smell of zinnias had reminded him of Gramps.

It was funny about smells. Livvie smelled of spring. Jim smelled of the woods. School smelled of wet galoshes and the sweeping compound the janitor sprinkled on the floor when he swept up. The house still smelled of Baba and Gramps. It would always be their house; their smells had soaked into it, the horehound jar and the camphorated oil, the naphtha soap and the cascara. On humid days there was a musty odor from the deer's head mounted above the mantle, a five-point buck that Gramps had killed the year before he died. The shot had gone right through the buck and killed the doe too. Gramps had felt bad about killing the doe.

"What's the difference, Gramps?" Robbie had said. "Buck or doe, killin' is killin', ain't it?"

"The doe carries life in her, Robbie," Gramps had replied. "You should always respect the doe, same as you'd respect your mother or your wife — "

125

A noise on the back porch roused Robbie from his half-sleep.

" 'Evenin', Madelyn. Odie 'n me'll be usin' your kitchen for a bit, if you don't mind."

"Make yourself at home, Stan. There's fresh coffee on the stove. Libby and I will be in the parlor — "

It was Stanfill P. Stanfill and Mr. Houtekier. Robbie slipped out of bed and put an ear to the grate.

"This won't take long, Odie. Now, the way I understand it, you were fixin' to get yourself a deer out of season — "

"But Stan — "

"Don't say a word, Odie! Not a word! Now, you'd just got down the gun when Miz Houtekier let out an awful scream. You ran in from the sunporch, and somehow the gun went off — "

Robbie's mind was too clouded with sleep to fully comprehend the implications of what he was hearing, but a great feeling of reassurance came over him. Sister Bay was looking after its own. All the sweet people!

He crawled back into bed and pulled the quilts up tight. They said Okie kids were starving in the Dust Bowl, and German kids were goose-stepping to school in short pants and Nazi brassards. But none of it seemed real. If it wasn't happening to you, it didn't seem real. Sister Bay had the lake and the woods and Stanfill P. Stanfill.

Everything would be all right.

21

In the morning, coming up the walk to Holy Childhood, with the day bright and lovely and church bells ringing, Robbie paused as a little procession of cars, five in all, drove by, the deputy's car in the lead and behind it the big black hearse carrying Wilma Houtekier's remains. It was remarkable, he thought, how quickly things got done when you died.

"She was your friend," a voice from behind him said, "wasn't she?"

Robbie turned around. It was Sister Joan Therese shepherding the mission children to mass.

"Yes, Sister," Robbie said. "She taught me about plants and things."

"She was good at that," Sister said, "giving little pieces of herself to others. I suppose that's what life's all about, giving little pieces of yourself to others."

The hearse turned up Bluff Road and went out of sight.

"You should be thankful, Robbie," Sister said. "You've had so many good friends. Light a candle for Wilma. A candle will help."

They started up to the church. The tall maples that lined the walk were turning a bright orange. Robbie liked going to mass on Sunday mornings. He liked the way the church bells rang and the way the little wooden church looked when you saw it in the distance, gray with white trim and a cross atop the steeple.

"They say trouble," Robbie said, "comes in threes."

"Sometimes it seems so, Robbie," Sister replied. "But if trouble comes in threes, so do good things. It all evens out."

The church was beginning to fill up. Organ music came from the choir loft. The mission children filed up the aisle and into the three front pews that were always reserved for them at the eight o'clock service. A few of them were giggling, but most were quiet and orderly with their hands piously folded. Indians had something special, Robbie thought, a pride, perhaps, or a sticking together. It showed in their eyes and in the sheen of their black hair.

Robbie walked to the front of the altar, genuflected, and then moved to the rack of candles under the statue of the Virgin Mary. He dropped a penny in the coin box and lit

128

one of the candles. The candle flickered brightly in its little red holder.

It was the wondering where they had gone that bothered you, he thought as he walked back down the aisle and slipped into a rear pew. You saw them in their caskets cold and waxen, and you wondered where they had gone. They had to have gone somewhere. It was unacceptable to think otherwise, no matter what the Swede said. Unacceptable and illogical. Nothing ever really died. You caught a fish and ate it, and the fish became you. The fish became literature and science and great music. And then when you died you became something else too. But *what?* And *where?*

There was a jangling of bells. Father Baumgarten and the altar boys came out from the sacristy, and mass began. Robbie tried to concentrate on his prayers, but his mind kept drifting. It didn't matter. Praying, he had learned from Sister Joan Therese, was a frame of mind.

He thought of Odie Houtekier and wondered what would become of him. He would sell the house, probably; all the children had married and moved away. That was how a town changed, Robbie supposed. Things happened. People were born and died. Others came and went. Old businesses failed and new ones were started up. There were new inventions, new songs, new hair styles, until pretty soon it was all changed. If you stayed, you didn't notice it much. It happened gradually, and you didn't notice it. But if you stayed, it was up to you to

129

preserve the character of the town, the idea of the town, so that even with all the changes it would still be the same kind of town. Only a few people, really, kept things going. Robbie would be one of them, and Jim too. They would make Loon Lodge a showcase, marketing their produce under a special label, *Loon Lodge Farm Products, Sister Bay, Wisconsin, U.S.A.*, with maybe a sketch of a loon coming in over the Up Holly. With Loon Lodge you could help keep it a good town the way Gramps would have liked. And then when your time came it wouldn't matter. Things would be straight in your mind, as Mrs. Houtekier had said, and it wouldn't matter.

When mass let out, people were arriving for the nine o'clock service. They clustered around the newsboy who had just come from the depot with the downstate papers. Robbie spotted Mr. Buhl in the crowd, and then Livvie, in a bright yellow dress and with her missal tucked under one arm.

"Well, it's finally come, Robbie," Henry Buhl said, pointing to the newspapers.

The headlines were the biggest Robbie had ever seen.

ALLIES DECLARE WAR ON GERMANY!
Hitler Rejects British Ultimatum;
Panzer Divisions Race Toward Warsaw!

Henry Buhl went on in to church; Livvie stayed behind with Robbie.

"Are you all right, Robbie?"

130

"I guess so. It's just there's been so much dyin' lately."

"Your Aunt Lib go home?"

"Uh-huh. On the local."

"Ma's gone down to Black River Falls with Mr. Houtekier. Pa says you can come up for dinner if you'd like."

"I don't think so, Livvie," Robbie said. "We're seein' Mr. Stanfill later on."

Livvie slipped her hand into Robbie's. "Please, Robbie," she whispered. "We're havin' stuffed pork chops."

"For cryin' out loud, Livvie!" Robbie said, irritably. "Can't a guy get a little peace?"

He pulled his hand away and started down the walk, then stopped and came back.

"I'm sorry, Livvie," he apologized.

"It's all right, Robbie," Livvie said. "Maybe you can come by after you see Mr. Stanfill."

"Yeah," Robbie said. "Maybe."

The organ music from inside the church swelled, and there was the shuffling of feet as the congregation rose for the beginning of mass.

Livvie turned and hurried up the steps, her head bent down to hide the tears that filled her eyes.

22

Violet Barrow had cranked down the striped awning at the Dew Drop Inn to shade the trays of fudge and pralines from the bright afternoon sun. Inside, the place smelled cool and sweet from all the ice cream. Stanfill P. Stanfill was talking about the war.

"There'll be no stopping them, Robbie." He was a stocky man with bushy eyebrows and a nice smile. He spoke in a slow drawl, deep and throaty, and there was a button missing from his vest. "Hitler'll flank the Maginot Line and be in Paris by spring."

"Or sooner," the Swede said.

"But what about England?" Robbie said.

"Oh, I imagine they'll put up a stiff enough fight," Mr. Stanfill said. "But some strange notions are loose over there, Robbie. Sooner or later it'll be up to us to stamp them out."

"I don't understand it," Robbie said. "Everybody says they don't want war, but we keep on havin' them."

"It's complicated, Robbie," the Swede said. "It's the leaders mostly. The leaders get peeved and start bickerin' 'mongst themselves."

Stanfill P. Stanfill had treated them to chocolate sodas. His straw made a slurping noise at the bottom of the glass.

"Oh-hh, I don't know, Swede," he said. "It's not all that complicated. The politicians tell you that to cover up their bunglin'. Shoot, the World War wasn't any more complicated than a squabble over butter prices. No, in my judgment everybody's to blame. Leaders reflect what's in the people."

"Then there's nothin' an ordinary person can do," Robbie said, "is there?"

"I suppose not, Robbie," Mr. Stanfill said, "except set an example in his own life. But then that's everything, isn't it?"

He took out a cigar and lit it. The blue-gray smoke trailed up and caught a little shaft of sunlight that came in through a tear in the awning.

"Well," he said, "you're not here to listen to me jabber about the war. Robbie, the Swede's told me about your suspicions. The Herr Doktor's an important man. You realize these are serious charges?"

For a second, Robbie felt a sinking sensation in his stomach.

"Yes, sir," he said.

Mr. Stanfill gave Robbie a long, stern look.

"We-ll," he said after a minute, "wouldn't surprise me a bit. And you think Edgar Bauer and Earl Dodson are mixed up in it too?"

"Yes, sir."

The Swede nudged Mr. Stanfill and pointed out the window.

"Lookit," he said, and grinned.

It was the Herr Doktor walking up Main Street past Burr's hardware, in his riding outfit as usual, breeches and a black turtleneck and shiny brown boots. Mr. Stanfill watched till he had gone out of sight.

"Arrogant little runt, ain't he?" the Swede said.

Stanfill P. Stanfill grunted. "I'd give my eyeteeth to catch that little Prussian peacock off base," he said. He brushed an ash from the lapel of his blue serge suit and returned to Robbie. "But — there are complications."

It was a funny case, he said. There was no conclusive evidence that Charlie had set the fire, but there wasn't a scrap of proof the Herr Doktor had done it either.

"But the candles 'n things the kids found in the *Arthur T.* . . . ," the Swede said.

"It ain't enough, Swede," Mr. Stanfill said. "The fact that a person possesses the means of setting a fire doesn't mean he actually set it."

He puffed quietly on his cigar for a moment.

"I think you're probably correct in your suspicions, Robbie," he said. "But right now we're up a blind alley. 'Course, if it really turns out there's another will — well, that's an equine of a different hue."

"A what?" Robbie said.

"A horse of a different color, Robbie," the Swede explained.

They all laughed. Stanfill P. Stanfill had a fine way about him, Robbie thought.

"But even the will is a will-o'-the-wisp, so to speak," Mr. Stanfill said. "I've talked to Sally Armitage. All she's got is a hunch, and that's not good enough."

"Couldn't you just go over to Moonrise and poke around, Stan?" the Swede asked.

"There're no grounds, Swede," Mr. Stanfill said. "Besides, I wouldn't know where to look. Sally said she's already searched high 'n low."

Suddenly Robbie felt a great agitation. There was something he had overlooked, he was convinced, some detail, some bit of information. And then he remembered. Wilma Houtekier's photo album. He told Mr. Stanfill about the tunnel that had run down to the beach.

"Yes, Robbie," the district attorney said. "I remember that tunnel. But it was filled in years ago."

"Well," Robbie said, "one day last spring when I was canoein' over to Moonrise, a rainstorm came up and I got drenched. Alvia was out in the summerhouse. She waved when she saw me comin' into the cove, and then when I got up to the house, she was waitin' with some towels to dry me off — ''

"So?" the Swede said.

"Well," Robbie said, "Alvia was dry."

"I don't follow you, Robbie," the Swede said.

"I do," Stanfill P. Stanfill said. "How did she get from the summerhouse to the mansion without getting wet?"

"You mean there's a second tunnel?"

"Apparently," Mr. Stanfill said.

"Couldn't you get a search warrant or somethin', Mr. Stanfill?" Robbie said.

"Nope, Robbie. Your say-so's not enough, and after twenty-six years as district attorney of Sawyer County I'm not about to start cutting corners with the law." He paused and fiddled with his cigar. "Of course, if a couple of enterprising kids were to snoop around over there — ''

"You mean you want us to do it?" Robbie said.

"I'm not suggesting you do a thing, Robbie", Mr. Stanfill said. "I'm just saying that — well, in matters of trespass minors enjoy a certain latitude that grownups don't . . .''

Robbie mulled over the possibilities. It would have to be Wednesday, he thought. The Herr Doktor went to town hall Wednesday nights, and Madelyn VanEpp would be having the Sodality over. He and Livvie were supposed to help with the harvest festival float, but they would make up a story and get excused. He would send smoke signals to Jim. Jim could hitchhike down from the reservation, then catch a lift up to Hayward on the creamery truck. They would take the *Ruby Allen*. No, the canoe would be quiet and more maneuverable. Besides, if they got caught, the *Ruby Allen* might implicate the Swede, and there'd be no end to it. It was funny how Mr. Stanfill had left the whole thing up to them.

"Stan has a way of doin' that, Robbie," the Swede said as they waved goodbye to Stanfill P. Stanfill and started up Main Street, "of placin' responsibility square on your shoulders."

They crossed over to Lydia's Five & Dime, where the Swede's truck was parked. A National Guard convoy was coming through town. They were on maneuvers. There had been stories in the *Record* about how they had to use sticks for guns and sacks of flour for bombs.

"The United States don't believe in war, Robbie," the Swede said. "That's why we never have much of an army."

They waved to the soldiers, and the soldiers waved back.

23

On a narrow finger of land that curved out into the lake to form a little cove, the red-slate roof of Moonrise gleamed in the sun.

Robbie paddled slowly around the point and into a clump of reeds to avoid being seen. The summerhouse, he could observe, had been shuttered up. Jim would have to bring his knife; they might have to pry the door.

He looked down the long line of Lombardy poplars to the Herr Doktor's place at the foot of the cove. Nothing. Then his eyes scanned the wide, sloping lawn of Moonrise for signs of activity. Nothing. He wondered who was taking care of the horses. He slouched back in the birch-bark canoe to wait, to try and detect a pattern of activity.

Moonrise was the most magnificent house Robbie had ever seen. There were twenty main rooms and a dozen smaller ones and a vestibule of beveled glass from Tiffany's in New York. Once, Alvia had taken him up to the big third-floor bedroom where there was a chimney with an oval stained-glass window instead of a fireplace. The glass played tricks with the curling smoke and turned the sunset into lovely patterns on the wall.

Robbie tilted his face to the warm sun and shut his eyes. Could all this really be happening?

He thought of the time he had come down with cat fever, when he was a little boy, and Alvia had come down from Moonrise with a goose-grease compress for his chest and a bedwarmer to make him sweat.

"If the fever isn't gone by morning," she had told his mother, "signal me on Hauger's bell."

In his delirium he had thought she was Florence Nightingale, pale and lovely with a cool hand on his brow.

It was a very special occasion, everybody had said, Alvia's coming down to look in on him. She hardly ever left Moonrise anymore. The Herr Doktor said she wasn't well, but there was speculation whether her mind had gone funny.

And then Robbie's thoughts went ahead to eighth grade. That was the year Sister Joan Therese had talked of stick-to-it-iveness and the fragility of relationships. There is a pattern, she had said, a glorious, divine pattern, and even our most insignificant actions have consequences that reverberate forever.

Robbie knew Sister was right, for if he hadn't fallen into a ravine at the powwow that year all the rest might never have happened.

He had come to lying face-down on the examining table up in the Herr Doktor's loft. He could feel Gerta Brandt, the Herr Doktor's nurse, holding him down.

"This is going to hurt, young man."

The pain had been stupifying. Afterward he had walked down to the Moonrise landing to splash water on his face.

"Yoo-hoo!"

He had looked up at the mansion. It was Alvia, very gay and coquettish in a white organdy dress, waving a handkerchief from the summerhouse.

"I've written a poem," she had said, taking a scrap of paper from her Pinafore box. "Would you like to hear it?"

> *'Tell me, at dawn do the lilacs call you*
> *Back to the pool where the cardinals sing?' "*

And she had put on a record and taught him how to waltz, and it wasn't till he was leaving that he realized she was very drunk.

"You musn't breathe a word, Robbie!" Mrs. Armitage had pleaded. "She's been under great stress."

"No, ma'am, I won't. She's a great lady."

And then last year he had started coming over every Monday and Friday, to help in the rose garden or clean the stables or shovel the snow, and each time Mrs. Armitage would give him a dollar from the household money.

140

"They laugh at her," she had said, "but they're beholden. All of them! Without her courage at the tannery this would be a ghost town."

Robbie sensed there was a special relationship between himself and Alvia, but he could not have defined it. But he knew it involved self-sacrifice and was — chaste.

And then there was the final memory of all, that night at Billy Sashabaw's lake, Alvia nude and knee-deep in the water and the Morgan horses stirring restlessly in the old Indian camp. Robbie had never seen a grown woman nude before. Alvia was past forty, he knew, but in the moonlight there was a smooth alabaster loveliness to her body. He wanted to stare at her, explore her, figure it all out —

But there had been no time for that. There had been only a great wildness and incoherence, and Alvia's anguished cries to the Winnebago gods, like a wolf baying at the moon.

> *"Tebeniminung!* . . . *Tebeniminung!* . . .
> *Teb-en-im-i-nunnng!* . . ."*

Somehow he had managed to get her back into her clothes and up on her horse. And as they started up the trail to Moonrise, Robbie had looked back at the Indian camp and the lake and felt a timeless bond with Billy Sashabaw.

24

It was fully dark when Jim shoved them off from the Buhls' pier. The lake was acting up. It had been a misty, overcast day, and now it was a dark, stormy night. The clouds were all right, Robbie thought; the clouds would shut out the moon. But a storm was something else.

"You sure picked a peach of a night for it, Robbie," Jim said as the canoe slapped precariously into the waves.

They paddled up past Hauger's Landing, keeping close to shore. Across the lake the lights of Moonrise flickered through the trees.

"Golly," Livvie said. "It's so dark I can't see a thing."

"Don't look straight at things, Livvie," Jim said. "Look a little to the side of them."

Robbie had planned it all very carefully. They would cross the lake well above Moonrise, then swing around behind Garbutt's Island and come down the eastern shore. Above Moonrise there was a stretch of hemlock woods, and above the woods a little meadow with an inlet that angled into it. They would leave the canoe in the shelter of the inlet and go the rest of the way on foot.

"What do you think, Jim?" Robbie said, looking up at the sky. "Will it get any worse?"

"Not likely," Jim said. "It should start to clear up soon."

"How can you tell, Jim?" Livvie said. She sat Indian-fashion behind Robbie, a kerosene lantern, unlighted, in her lap and a handful of stove matches tucked in the pocket of her dirndl dress.

"It's in the air, Livvie," Jim said. "The air smells drier."

Robbie backwatered to hold the canoe steady. He looked across the lake. The lights of Moonrise had disappeared from view.

"Okay," he said. "Let's go."

He drew a deep breath and swung them out into the lake. The whitecapped waves looked cold and frosty as they crashed against the canoe.

"Keep exactly in the middle, Livvie," he ordered, "so's we stay in balance."

They paddled hard across the lake. The wind hollowed

out their cheeks and stung their eyes. Livvie gripped the lantern between her legs and held tight to the gunwales. Twice Robbie nearly lost his paddle, and once Jim fell forward onto Livvie when his paddle missed the water.

Robbie was filled with misgivings. It was all wrong, he thought. After all the planning and preparation, it was all wrong. Their attitude was wrong, the fibbing to get out of harvest festival was wrong, the weather was wrong. There was a certain integrity to all successful endeavors, he knew, a confidence and unity of purpose. Somehow they had lost it. It was their breaking the law, he supposed. It didn't feel right, breaking the law. He had learned from living close to the land that there was a balance to things, even intangible things, as if everything in the universe were in a fixed supply that could neither be increased nor diminished. Nothing was ever gained without something's being lost. No one was rich without someone's being poor on account of it. There was no good luck without someone else's misfortune. Breaking the law was even more clear-cut. If you got caught, you got punished. If you got away with it, there was guilt. But either way you paid the price. There was no getting around the price.

"We should've worn slickers," Livvie said, shivering, her hair wet from the spray of the waves. "It'd be warmer with slickers."

"It'll be all right once we get out of the wind," Jim said. "It's the wind that makes it cold."

Robbie set a course by the lights of Garbutt's Island, but

when they swung behind the island he was left with only his instincts and knowledge of the lake to bring them ashore at the correct point. He could smell the hemlocks before he could make out the shoreline, and even then he nearly missed the inlet.

"To starboard, Robbie!" Jim called out as the canoe scraped against a dead tree that had fallen out into the water. "Quick!"

The inlet was quiet and sheltered. The moon broke through the clouds briefly as they secured the canoe. Jim led them up the bank and into the hemlock woods. Robbie's spirits were improving. Jim was right; it was clearing. Dry air was moving in, and the pressure was rising. You always felt better when the pressure went up.

"Keep your head bent down, Livvie," Jim said. "There's a lot of low-hanging branches."

They came out of the hemlock woods opposite the Moonrise stables and stood there crestfallen.

"Oh, no!" Jim groaned.

Below them, at the end of a wide expanse of lawn, lights were shining brightly from the main floor of the mansion, and the Herr Doktor's white Lincoln Zephyr was parked under the portico. As they stood there they heard the sound of an approaching car, then saw headlights moving through the woods at the foot of the cove, where the private Moonrise road crossed an old logging trail. The car came up the cobblestone driveway and pulled up under the portico. It was Edgar Bauer in the tannery station wagon.

"What d'you think happened, Robbie?" Jim said. "The town meetin' wouldn't be over this early."

"I don't know, Jim," Robbie said. "I guess he didn't go."

"Oh, it's ruined!" Livvie said, half crying. "And after all that trouble!"

"Maybe not," Robbie said. "It depends on the moon. We could probably get into the summerhouse okay, but if it clears up they might spot us on the way out."

"What then?" Jim said.

"We'd just have to make a break for it," Robbie replied.

They agreed that if anything went wrong Jim and Livvie would make their way back to the canoe while Robbie diverted their pursuers down the old logging trail.

"C'mon," Robbie said. "I'll lead the way."

They moved out of the woods and started down to the mansion. The moon had come out again, and the wind seemed to be dying down. They could hear the Morgan horses whinnying in their stalls.

"Oh, Robbie!" Livvie whispered. "I'm scared!"

When Robbie was a little boy he had heard many stories about how Moonrise had been in its heyday, about the parties the Senator had held when Alvia was a belle, grand affairs with croquet and morris-dancing and a string ensemble brought up all the way from the Palmer House in Chicago. Important people from the North Shore would be invited up, as well as Alvia's fancy friends from out East. At night there would be Japanese lanterns and

146

Mumm's champagne, and lovely Strauss waltzes would fill the soft summer air.

And now, as they worked their way down to the cove and circled around behind the summerhouse, trespassing and about to commit burglary, Robbie felt a great sadness for the way things had ended up. Alvia was dead, and already there were signs of neglect and disrepair. The grass needed cutting, and a door in the stables hung off its hinges. He wondered what had made Alvia end up the way she had, what had driven the Herr Doktor to sacrifice Charlie to further his own schemes. He had always thought things would be different for him and Jim and Livvie, that somehow they were very special, and that they would be able to carry the values and the goals of their youth into adulthood. But maybe it was not allowed. Maybe you reached a point where life bent you to its own purposes, and your hopes and dreams all melted away.

Then he remembered something Alvia had said one day in the rose garden.

"There's a sadness to life, Robbie, and in the end only a few people matter."

Robbie looked back at Jim and Livvie, the dear friends of his childhood. It occurred to him that Livvie looked particularly lovely when she was frightened, and he felt a strong impulse to pull her close and protect her forever. He imagined how it would be at Loon Lodge, at night, in their bedroom, Livvie's lean body close to his and her long chestnut hair fallen down over her bare shoulders. There would be her sweet whisperings, and moonlight on the pillows. Maybe, after all, there was some special instruction in the trouble of the past few weeks. Maybe if you were aware of the pitfalls you could avoid them. With Loon Lodge maybe you could gather the people that mattered close to you, and everything would be all right. Just maybe —

Around the south wing of Moonrise the wide windows of a solarium looked out over a terraced rose garden. At the end of the rose garden sat the shuttered summerhouse, like a doll's house, with a cupola and a mansard roof and a silver weather vane that spun in the wind. Robbie slipped from behind the summerhouse and looked up at the solarium. He could see three figures moving about, the Herr Doktor, Edgar Bauer, and Mr. Dodson. The door to the summerhouse was bolted but not locked. They slipped inside one by one while Robbie kept an eye on the sky for any break in the clouds that might expose them to the bright moonlight. Inside, the summerhouse was pitch black.

"Stand perfectly still," Robbie whispered to Jim and Livvie, "while I check the shutters."

He latched the door securely behind him, then groped his way around the familiar room, examining the shutters for cracks or openings that would let the light through.

"Okay, Livvie," he said when he was sure it was safe. "You can light the lantern."

Livvie felt in the dark for a place to strike a match. The lantern cast a soft light over the room and its furnishings, wicker chairs and tables, mostly, and lamps with tasseled shades. Jim had already located the trap door, under a large oriental rug in the center of the floor. The door was warped shut. Jim pried it open with his hunting knife.

"It's a stairway," he said, peering down into the opening.

Robbie led the way down. There was a long arched passageway, limestone, maybe, or ledgerock, that ran in the direction of the house. Cobwebs hung from the ceiling, and there was a dank, musty smell. A clutter of old furniture lined the walls, as with an attic. Robbie pushed a faded dressmaker's form out of the way and walked quickly to the other end. There was a second stairway, this one leading up into the house.

"Near as I can figure," he said, "it comes out under the staircase in the main entrance hall."

The lantern made distorted shadows on the walls. Robbie had a closed-in feeling.

"C'mon," he said, "we don't have much time. Jim, you start at that end. We'll work from both directions."

Jim grinned. "Shoot," he said, "I already found it."

He pointed to a glass-doored bookcase that was wedged behind an old steamer trunk. A brightly colored object glittered from the top shelf.

"That's it!" Robbie said.

Jim got the music box from the bookcase and set it on the trunk. It was a large box with quilted material on the sides and a gay Victorian scene sketched on the lid, with young men in frock coats and pretty girls with parasols strolling along a river. Robbie felt his heart racing as he pressed a little button and raised the lid. There was a whirring noise, and then a little tune tinkled through the passageway.

"It's from the operetta," Livvie said. "We did it for May festival last year." She remembered the lyrics and sang them in a whisper.

> *"Let the air with joy be laden,*
> *Rend with songs the air above,*
> *For the union of a maiden,*
> *With the man who owns her love."*

Robbie rummaged through the Pinafore box. The box was crammed with dance cards and souvenirs and scraps of paper with poems scrawled on them. There were two stubs from the Zigfeld Theater in New York and a yellowed photograph of a young man in an aviator's helmet. A verse had been written on the back.

> *Remember the day*
> *The Eleventh went up,*
> *And never came back?*
> *Oh, me!*

"That's Hubert Locke," Robbie said, handing the photo to Livvie. "He was Alvia's beau."

Livvie looked at the picture and gasped. "Robbie! He looks just like you!"

"Yeah," Robbie said. "I know."

Livvie read the verse and sighed. "It must have been

so sad,'' she said. ''I think I'm beginning to understand Alvia.''

Robbie's heart sank when he worked down to the bottom of the box without finding anything.

''Looks like we're out of luck,'' he said.

Then he felt a bulge in the satin lining under the lid of the box. He worked the lining loose and pulled out a long brown envelope with the imprint of an Eau Claire law firm in the corner.

LAST WILL AND TESTAMENT
Alvia Bartholomew Ivors
August 15, 1939

''Quick, Livvie!'' he said. ''Hold the lantern closer.''

He opened the envelope and took out the will. The document was typed on several sheets of stiff paper with red margins running down the sides. He skimmed the first page, then the second, and then broke into a wide smile.

''Mrs. Armitage!'' he said. ''Mrs. Armitage inherits it all!''

They all began jumping up and down. But their elation turned to fear when they heard voices up in the summerhouse. There was a commotion and then the sound of footsteps on the stairway. For a second they stood there frozen. Then Robbie stuffed the envelope in Jim's shirt and grabbed the lantern.

''Quick!'' he whispered. ''We'll have to get out through the house.''

They raced to the end of the passageway and started up the stairs to the house.

"You'n Livvie make a beeline for the canoe," Robbie whispered to Jim. "I'll let 'em catch sight of me, then head for the old logging trail."

The voices behind them were growing more distinct now, and there was a loud clicking noise, sharp and metallic, as with rifles being cocked. Livvie reached for Robbie's hand and held it tight.

"Be careful, Robbie!" she whispered. "I think they've got guns."

25

Robbie ran hard down the old logging trail. The trail was sandy in spots. Twice he slipped in the sand and fell. The sand was no good, he thought; the sand made it slow going.

He looked back up the trail. The clouds had shut out the moon again. He was safe now. Even if they caught up to him it would be too dark for the rifles. At first there had been three of them, but the pace had been too much for Mr. Dodson. Robbie had made sure the Herr Doktor and Edgar Bauer had seen him turn off onto the logging trail, but now there was no sign of them. Perhaps they had given up. It didn't matter; Livvie and Jim would have reached the canoe by now. He wondered what had gone wrong back at Moonrise. They couldn't have heard them talking; the passageway was deep underground. It had to have been the lantern. He had overlooked a knothole or a crack in the shutters, and they had seen the light.

He started back down the trail. When he heard the rushing sound of the Narrows, he slowed to a walk. The trail ended at an impassable thicket of rocks and brambles. On one side a rocky incline led straight down to the Narrows; the other side broke away in flat marshland that ran a mile or so to the Soo Line tracks. He would cross the marsh, then follow the tracks back to town. The marsh would be wet and muddy, but the Narrows was too treacherous to swim.

Suddenly he stopped. Sounds were coming from behind him, different sounds than before. He turned to look just as the glow of two lanterns materialized around a bend in the trail. It was the Herr Doktor and Edgar Bauer on horses. Their rifle barrels showed clearly in the light of the lanterns. So they hadn't given up the chase after all; they had simply gone back to get the horses. There would be no time for the marsh now; the marsh would be too slow. They would catch him for sure — or shoot him.

The horses were less than a hundred yards away and coming at a trot. Robbie hurried to the end of the trail and started down the steep bank to the Narrows, half sliding at times and breaking his descent by grabbing hold of the pine saplings that grew through the rocks. Downstream, he could make out the pilings of the old trestle, with the current surging around them. Perhaps he should pick a spot farther upstream; it would lessen his chances of being smashed against the pilings. But the Herr Doktor and Edgar Bauer would be on him in a minute. Besides, he was anxious for the challenge. Nobody had ever swum the Narrows when it was running hard. Livvie and Jim would be flabbergasted, and the farm ladies at Arbuckle's would whisper, *"There goes the VanEpp kid. He's the one that swam the Narrows."*

He experienced the sensation of flight as his body arched out over the channel, then the cold slap of the water. The coldness of the water took his breath away. He swam upstream at an angle to avoid the pilings. The clouds still blotted out the moon, but he could make out the opposite bank. He swam hard, the hissing, rushing, foaming sound of the Narrows all around him.

Halfway across he began to angle downstream, letting the current veer him in toward shore. It was easy, he thought, disappointingly easy, even with his clothes weighting him down. It was a myth about the Narrows being so treacherous. Next summer he and Jim would —

He never completed the thought. He had hit a whirl-pool. In an instant he was sucked under, swirling, tumbling, pitching, like water glugging down a drain. Water went up his nose and left a tingling pressure in his forehead. He struggled to get his bearings in the black water. Don't fight it, he told himself. Ride with the current. But his heart was pounding, and his lungs felt ready to burst.

Then one of his hands struck something hard and slimy. Had the current carried him into the pilings? He felt a dull thump on his head, then a snapping sensation in his neck — not pain, just a loud snap followed by an explosion of colors. Everything seemed to slow down. He felt nauseous and confused. Was his number up? He should have gone farther upstream. It was his pride, his sinful pride, and his conceit. He had underestimated everything. He had underestimated the Herr Doktor. He had underestimated the Narrows and its capabilities. You had to respect nature to survive in it, but he had failed to respect the Narrows, and now it was claiming him as its own. He pictured the Swede and his father fishing his bloated body from the reeds with grappling hooks. The town would give him a fine funeral and bury him in the cemetery overlooking the bay.

Then suddenly he realized it wasn't pretending, that he was seconds away from death. A frustrated anger built up in him. He didn't want to die. He never wanted to die. There were so many good things in life, tastes and smells and things to see and touch. It would take a couple of lifetimes to get around to them all. A thousand years wouldn't be enough. Then a vision of Livvie flashed before his eyes, in a bright yellow dress and with her missal tucked under one arm, coming up the walk to Holy Childhood. He wouldn't be cheated out of it, of Livvie and Loon Lodge and moonlight on the pillows. He just wouldn't.

Then a thin eerie light filtered from the direction he had thought was bottom. The moon had come out again. He somersaulted around, his sense of equilibrium restored,

156

and as he did so his feet touched bottom. He bent his knees and gave a mighty shove, summoning up every bit of strength that was left in him. He did it calmly and deliberately, working his arms in long, powerful strokes. He broke the surface, gulping for air. The cool night wind hit his face like a tonic. But it wasn't enough. The current still had him. He flailed wildly, his arms heavy as lead, till finally he made a tremendous lurch and broke free. It was a fine feeling! It was the finest feeling he had ever experienced. He started to let out a whoop, then remembered the Herr Doktor and Edgar Bauer.

He sidestroked into calmer waters, letting the current carry him downstream. Below the pilings there was a willow tree with a grassy spot beneath it. He crawled ashore and collapsed in the cool, sweet-smelling grass, his clothes dripping and his hair matted down over his eyes. A frog croaked from somewhere. It was funny, he thought, the effect danger had on you. There was fear but exhilaration too. His body was bone tired, but his senses were keen and alert.

He lay there for several minutes resting and trying to prolong his sensations. Up the lake, lights were still burning at Garbutt's Island. It couldn't be too late. He would toss pebbles up at Livvie's window, maybe, or go on up to the Swede's. It wouldn't do for him to go home a mess. He wished his father were home; his father would be proud of him.

He climbed up the bank and started up the lake. When the shoreline opened on the main body of the upper arm, he cut inland to the path he and Jim used when they fished the Narrows for bullheads. It was slow going. Clouds kept shutting out the moon. He groped in the dark to find his way, waving a stick in front of him as he had seen blind men do. The wind had picked up. He began to shiver. He wished he could take off his wet clothes.

When the path curved around a large oak tree, he knew he was just below the Buhls' pasture. He broke into a run to keep warm, his shoes squishing and his wet pants legs flapping noisily. Then he saw a lantern flickering through the trees and stopped dead in his tracks. Maybe the Herr Doktor and Edgar Bauer had spotted him swimming the Narrows and had come across the lake by boat. Or maybe they had spotted Jim and Livvie in the canoe. Maybe the whole escapade had come apart.

He ducked into the brush and crouched low. Then two unmistakable forms loomed out of the shadows.

"Livvie!" Robbie hollered, stepping out into the path. "Swede!"

Livvie let out a yell, then ran down the path ahead of the Swede.

"Oh, Robbie, Robbie, Robbie!" she cried, throwing her arms around him. "I was so worried!"

"But how the heck — "

"We saw the Herr Doktor and Edgar Bauer get the horses," Livvie explained. "Jim figured your only chance would be to swim the Narrows."

"Did Jim make the creamery truck?"

"Uh-huh," Livvie said with a giggle. "With ten sec-

158

onds to spare. He's going to leave the will in Mr. Stanfill's mailbox.''

The Swede clomped noisily out of the darkness, holding a lantern high and with an army blanket slung over one shoulder.

"Holy mackerel!" he bellowed, taking the blanket from his shoulder and wrapping it around Robbie. "You look like a soggy sack of seaweed!"

"Hello, Swede," Robbie grinned, his teeth chattering. "We found the will."

"So I heard." The Swede shook Robbie's hand and slapped him on the back. "C'mon, 'fore you catch your death. I've got a fire goin' and some cider warmin'.''

Livvie smiled happily.

"Oh, isn't it wonderful?" she cried, jumping up and down. "We found the will, and Robbie swam the Narrows, and now Charlie won't have to go to Mendota!"

"Not exactly, Livvie," the Swede said. "All it does is give Mr. Stanfill grounds to start building the same circumstantial case against the Herr Doktor that the Herr Doktor cooked up against Charlie."

"Oh phooey, Swede!" Livvie said. "Everything's going to be all right. I can *feel* it."

They hiked out of the woods and across the pasture, threading their way around the cowpies. Robbie huddled up in the blanket, his teeth chattering and his shoes squishing. The sky was clear now and the moon shone bright above them. The Swede led the way with the lantern. Livvie skipped along beside Robbie, holding her dress

down against the wind that blew up off the lake. Robbie
let the Swede get a little ways ahead of them, then pulled
Livvie close.

"Livvie?"

"Yes, Robbie?"

"I'm never going to leave you."

Livvie looked up at him with glistening eyes.

"Really and truly, Robbie?" she said softly.

"Really and truly. We're going to build Loon Lodge
and raise our family there and never leave Sister Bay."

"Oh, Robbie!" Livvie sighed. "I've been prayin'
you'd make the commitment."

"The commitment?" Robbie said. "But I don't understand — "

"Never mind, silly." Livvie reached up and kissed
him lightly on the lips, then snuggled in under the blanket. "We'll talk about it when your teeth stop chattering."

Robbie was overwhelmed with good feelings. Livvie
Buhl was his love, and she had come down the lake to find
him. He was Robin Hood and Beowulf and Sir Galahad
returned from the fray. And when the Swede swung into
one of his lumberjack tunes, Robbie sang out loudest of
all.

> *"My name is Yon Yonson,*
> *I come from Wisconsin,*
> *I work in a lumbermill there — "*

"Look, Robbie," Livvie said, pointing to the corn

160

shocks in the field above the pasture. "Aren't they lovely?"

Robbie looked up at the sloping cornfield. The corn shocks looked shadowy and lifelike against the moon-filled sky.

"Jim says corn shocks are really tepees, and that Injun spirits come back this time of year and dance under the moon."

"They don't really, Livvie," Robbie said. "That's just a superstition."

"I know," Livvie said, wistfully. "But it's nice to think they do. Sometimes make-believe things are truer than real things."

They sang all the way up to the Swede's, and their voices echoed out over the lake.

26

Robbie stayed close to the house the next day, waiting for something to happen, but the morning passed uneventfully. After lunch, Madelyn VanEpp walked down to Lydia's Five & Dime for some thread.

"Wasn't anybody talkin' or anything?" Robbie asked when she got back.

"Not a whisper," his mother replied. "Don't be surprised, son, if the Herr Doktor wheedles out of it. The rich have their little tricks."

Robbie was itching to go down to Arbuckle's and pick up the gossip, but he was afraid of running into the Herr Doktor. Throughout the whole business he had not thought of the Herr Doktor as a person but rather as a force, a sinister force that was threatening Charlie. It was easier to fight a force than a person.

The afternoon wore on. Finally, Millie Horton came by from the telephone office.

"Stanfill P. Stanfill called, Robbie," she said. "He wants to see you 'n Livvie up in his office. The Swede's comin' down to pick you up."

Millie eyed him suspiciously.

"You're not in any trouble, are you, Robbie?" she said.

Robbie's heart sank. If Millie hadn't heard anything, perhaps something had gone wrong.

The Swede had already been up to the courthouse.

"Stan's in a real pickle," he said after they had picked up Livvie and started up to Hayward.

"How do you mean, Swede?" Livvie said.

"Well, Livvie, the plain fact is he don't have much of a case. He figures Judge Koontz'll toss him out on his ear if he tries to take it into court."

"Shoot," Robbie said, "don't he realize by now Charlie's really innocent?"

"Oh, it ain't that, Robbie," the Swede said. "Stan did a little sleuthin' 'n figured the whole scheme out. Seems the Herr Doktor 'n Edgar Bauer was in cahoots to keep the tannery in bad financial shape so's Alvia'd be forced to sell out. They was submittin' high bids on government contracts, that sort of thing, and then when that didn't work they arranged the fire, timin' it to happen right after the new electric flesher'd been installed. They figured they'd just blame it on Charlie and nobody'd bat an eye."

163

"But what about the will, Swede?" Livvie said.

"Well, that's a little complicated too, Livvie," the Swede said. "Stan figures the Herr Doktor'll challenge it in court, probably try to make out that Alvia wasn't in her right mind when she made it. It could tie things up for a year or more. Meantime, the Herr Doktor'd be legally in control of things."

"So what's going to happen?" Robbie said.

"We-ll, Stan's goin' to play a little game of cat 'n mouse. You see, he snooped around and discovered the Herr Doktor never bothered to take out his final citizenship papers — "

"Holy cow!" Livvie said. "You mean he's not a citizen?"

"Not exactly, Livvie. But he ain't a full citizen."

"So?" Robbie said.

"So Stan's goin' to threaten him with a charge of arson unless he relinquishes his claim on Alvia's estate. Stan says he'll probably refuse. Then Stan'll threaten to take action with the immigration authorities and have the Herr Doktor deported as an undesirable alien."

"Can they do that?" Robbie asked.

"They can when you're not a full citizen, Robbie," the Swede replied. "Stan figures the Herr Doktor'll try 'n pressure him to back off, maybe shut down the tannery 'n and get the town all riled up."

"And then?" Livvie said.

"And then the two of 'em will sit down 'n dicker. If it goes the way Stan hopes it will, the Herr Doktor'll plead guilty to some sort of reduced charge. Then the new will will be certified, and Stan will drop the immigration business, and that will be that.''

"What about Edgar Bauer 'n Mr. Dodson?'' Robbie asked.

"Ain't you heard?'' the Swede said. "Both of 'em hightailed it out of town. That's Stan's trump card, the fact that they ran.''

It was almost closing time when they pulled up at the courthouse.

"You kids go on in by yourselves,'' the Swede said. "This is your show.''

Robbie felt a great sense of awe as he and Livvie climbed the worn courthouse steps and were ushered into Stanfill P. Stanfill's office. The office was gray and dusty. There were a few wooden chairs and a cuspidor and an old leather couch. One wall was lined with law books; an old pendulum clock hung from the opposite wall and below it a framed quotation:

Important principles may and must be inflexible.
             — Abraham Lincoln

"Robbie!'' It was Mrs. Armitage. "Livvie! Oh, Alvia would've been so proud!''

A tall young man with a tanned face came forward and extended his hand.

"This is my nephew Tom, Robbie,'' Mrs. Armitage said. "He's with the forest rangers over in the Flambeau.

He'll be running the tannery once things are straightened out."

Robbie took an immediate liking to Tom Armitage.

"Good luck, sir," he said.

"Thank you, Robbie," Tom Armitage said. "It will be nip and tuck for a while, but I think we can manage to keep things afloat."

Stanfill P. Stanfill, smiling, came from behind his desk and put his arms around Robbie and Livvie.

"Well, you kids've really stirred it up." He waved them onto the leather couch. "Understand you got a little wet last night, Robbie."

Robbie grinned. "A little," he said.

"Who was it dropped that envelope off at my house in the dead of night?" Mr. Stanfill asked.

"Jim Stillwater," Robbie said, and explained the events of the previous night.

"Well, I'll be danged!" the district attorney exclaimed. "A regular military operation — canoes and creamery trucks and diversionary tactics."

They talked excitedly for several minutes, and then Stanfill P. Stanfill turned to Sally Armitage and became serious.

"Sally," he said, "now that she's finally found peace of mind, I'd like to know what made a fine woman like Alvia Ivors go to pieces the way she did."

"Sooner or later life will break your heart, Stan," Sally Armitage replied. "It just happened to Alvia sooner than most."

166

And in the waning afternoon light she talked of Alvia and Moonrise and Billy Sashabaw. It all might have been different, she said, if Alvia's mama and papa had lived, but then who was to know? Junior was such a wastrel and his hussy of a wife no better. The child had been so alone, hanging on Billy Sashabaw's every word, and then, later, finding true love with Hubert Locke only to have it shattered by the war.

"You were a great joy to her this past year, Robbie," Sally Armitage said. "Part of her saw Hubert Locke in you, and another part saw the son she never had."

"What ever happened to Billy Sashabaw, Mrs. Armitage?" Livvie asked.

"Oh, it was one of those senseless squabbles, Livvie," Sally Armitage said. "One night the Senator came on Billy and Alvia over at that lake. Alvia was standing out in the water naked as a jaybird. She was a grown girl by that time, about your age, Livvie. Well — there was a terrible row. The Senator accused Billy of abusing Alvia, but it wasn't true. Billy worshipped that girl. But he felt humiliated by the Senator's nasty accusations, and so he left and never came back. Arthur Ivors was a good man but he came down too hard on Alvia. He was terribly possessive with her. She was all he had left, you see, and he lived in dread of the day she might leave him."

"Didn't anybody ever see Billy again?" Livvie said.

"No, Livvie. After the Senator died, Alvia was beside herself, and so she went up and down the Soo Line for weeks searching for Billy — "

"But she never found him?"

"Not exactly, Livvie," Sally Armitage said. "It turned out Billy had been trapping up along the St. Croix River. One night he got drunk and froze to death in the snow."

Nobody said anything for a long while. Outside, the setting sun cast long shadows on the courthouse lawn. There was the ticking of the pendulum clock and the clatter of a distant typewriter and the hollow sound of footsteps out in the corridor. Then Livvie said:

"Then it was the Senator's fault, all Alvia's unhappiness?"

"Not really, Livvie," Sally Armitage said, quietly. "It was like everything in life, I suppose, everybody's fault and nobody's fault."

The door to the office opened. Mr. Stanfill's secretary came in and whispered something in his ear.

"We-ll," he said, getting to his feet, "it appears the Herr Doktor has arrived." He gestured toward a door that opened directly on the corridor: "I think it'd be best if you all went out this way. Robbie, you wait outside. You'll have to make a statement and sign it."

"What about Charlie, Mr. Stanfill?" Robbie asked.

"He'll be released as soon as I can round up the sheriff, Robbie," Mr. Stanfill said. "I'll run him down to Sister Bay myself."

Mrs. Armitage hugged Robbie and Livvie.

"You can start picking out your things," she said, "as soon as it's all settled about the will."

"Our things?" Robbie said, puzzled.

168

"You mean you don't know?" Stanfill P. Stanfill said. "I sort of assumed you'd snuck a look at that will, Robbie."

"I did," Robbie said. "At least the part about Mrs. Armitage."

"Oh, there's more to it than that, Robbie," Mr. Stanfill said. "There's a codicil about you kids."

"A codicil?" Livvie said.

"A provision, Livvie," Mr. Stanfill said, "for your farm on the Up Holly. Alvia left the four of you the Morgan horses plus your pick of the equipment and furnishings: tools, furniture, anything you'd like."

Robbie and Livvie sat on a bench out in the corridor, trying to absorb what had happened. Livvie's eyes were filled with tears.

"Oh, I feel so guilty, Robbie," she said. "I was thinking such awful things about Alvia."

"She was a great lady, Livvie."

They were still sitting there when the door to Mr. Stanfill's office opened and the Herr Doktor came out. Robbie looked for an avenue of retreat, but the Herr Doktor had already seen him and was coming across the corridor. Robbie stood up, his heart pounding.

"It was you in the summerhouse?"

"Yes, sir," Robbie said.

"I should have known." He spoke in a slow, stilted manner with a heavy accent. "I used to see you in the rose garden. Once when you were younger, I stitched up a gash in your head. You had fallen into a ravine."

"Yes, sir, I remember."

"There was a little girl with you. She cried because she thought you were going to die." He gestured to Livvie. "This is the same girl?"

"Yes, sir," Robbie said. "Olivia Buhl."

"I see, I see," the Herr Doktor nodded. "It is good you have stayed together."

He gazed absently over Robbie's shoulder.

"I was like you when I was a boy. I climbed mountains and swam rivers. But — things change. We make trades, we make bargains, and in the end people mistake what we have become for what we are."

He sighed wearily.

"Well — we shall see," he said, and started to leave. "Yes, we shall see — "

And as he walked down the corridor and out of the courthouse, slowly, his head bent down, he no longer seemed haughty and arrogant.

"He's disgraced, Robbie," said Stanfill P. Stanfill, who had watched the little scene from his office door. "Disgrace is the worst form of punishment."

Robbie felt his lips quivering. He turned to the wall to hide his face. For the first time he understood about Sister Joan Therese's consequences. He made a fist and pounded the wall till his hand hurt.

27

And so it was over. Trouble had come and gone. Now there would be time for more normal pursuits. For the first time Robbie realized how thoroughly the business with Charlie had absorbed his energies. It was no good, he thought, when you concentrated on one thing too long.

"It's funny how it is when trouble's over," he said to the Swede on the drive back down to Sister Bay. "You feel relieved, but there's a letdown too."

"It's that way with most things, Robbie," the Swede said. "Best thing is to put your nose to the grindstone."

Livvie talked excitedly about Alvia's bequest.

"I don't think we'd want any of the furniture," she

said. "It wouldn't look right in Loon Lodge. And maybe we ought to just borrow the tools 'n things, then give them back to Mrs. Armitage when we get our own. What d'you think we should do about the Morgans, Swede?"

"Sellin' 'em would be the most sensible thing, Livvie," the Swede said. "A horse ain't much use round a farm 'cept for plowin', but plowin' ain't fit work for a Morgan. Certain animals have a dignity to 'em. Pity Alvia didn't have a tractor."

"Would they bring a good price?"

"The Morgans? Oh, they'd bring a fine price. You could buy a good plow horse and a few Guernseys and still have a little cash for seed 'n things."

The truck came around the line of hills where Big Chetac came into view. The lake was blue and choppy. Over on the Up Holly the Loon Lodge sign glinted in the sun.

"Oh, I just can't believe it!" Livvie exclaimed. "We're rich!"

"For a fact," the Swede said. "A lot richer'n you think, Livvie."

That evening, they all gathered in front of Holy Childhood to welcome Charlie home — Robbie and his mother, Livvie and the Swede, Violet and Mrs. Barrow, and Sister Joan Therese. It had been the Swede's idea that they meet at the church.

"But I thought you didn't believe in churches," Sister Joan Therese chided the Swede.

"Oh, it ain't a matter of belief, Sister," the Swede replied. "Church is a good thing on its own account."

172

It was nearly dark when Stanfill P. Stanfill's car came down Bluff Road and pulled up in front of the church. Charlie seemed a little unsteady on his feet. He waved as Mr. Stanfill drove off and then started up the walk. He looked tired and thin, and his arms windmilled about. In his haste, he stumbled and fell. Robbie started down to help him, but the Swede grabbed his arm.

"Let him do it by himself, Robbie," he said.

Charlie got to his feet and brushed off his overalls, and then, with a great effort to control the erratic movements of his body, he broke into a little run.

"Hey, h-h-hey on the midway!" he called to them, waving, with a grin on his face.

"He has the grace," Robbie heard Sister Joan Therese whisper. "That poor sick boy has the grace."

Then everybody broke out clapping.

"Move it or lose it, Charlie!" Robbie hollered.

"Drive it or milk it!" the Swede bellowed.

They all crowded around Charlie, laughing and talking excitedly.

"My Charlie's back!" Mrs. Barrow cried, hugging her son to her. She took a handkerchief from the pocket of her faded housedress and wiped her eyes. "Violet made you some batter bread, love," she said, "and there's leg o' lamb for supper."

"I'll have to g-g-get up early," Charlie grinned, "and d-d-dig some worms."

"No you won't, Charlie," Livvie said. "Robbie kept your worms for you, and dug some fresh ones besides."

As they started in to church, Millie Horton hurried up the walk.

"There's a call for you at the phone office, Madelyn," she said to Robbie's mother. "It's Nate."

Robbie felt a flutter of excitement run through him. It would be his father, he thought, calling to let them know what train he would be on.

"Can I go with you, Mom?"

"No, it wouldn't be polite to Charlie, Robbie," Madelyn VanEpp said. "You wait here with the others. I won't be long."

The church was dark except for the glow of the vigil candles. They filed into a pew in front of the statue of the Virgin Mary. It was nice in the church in the semidarkness, Robbie thought. Certain buildings seemed to take on special qualities from the character of their use. The little wooden church would always be a church, as if all the praying and genuflecting had been absorbed into its timbers.

Sister Joan Therese led them in prayer.

"Lord, we give thanks for the safe return of Charlie Barrow . . ."

When Madelyn VanEpp returned, she signaled to Robbie to come outside.

"Come on, Livvie," Robbie whispered.

It was a bright night, and a cool wind was coming up off the bay.

"What is it, Mom?" Robbie asked.

"Your father won't be coming home right away," Ma-

174

delyn VanEpp said. There was a worried look on her face. "He got the job at Inland Tool."

Robbie stood there in disbelief.

"But I thought they'd turned him down," he said.

"It's the war, Robbie," Madelyn VanEpp said. "There are more jobs on account of the war."

"Oh, Robbie!" Livvie whispered. She took his hand and held it tight.

"He's rented a place on the west side with an option to buy," Madelyn VanEpp said. "He wants you to go down and help him fix it up. The coal-bin needs repairing and there's some painting and wallpapering to do."

Robbie looked down at the bay. It was finished, he thought. All of it. Loon Lodge and the blue herons and the sweet smells of the Narrows.

"I'm sorry, Robbie," Madelyn VanEpp said. "I tried."

She reached out to her son, but Robbie pulled away.

"It's not fair!" he said, his lips set tight. "It's just not fair!"

He turned and started across the church lawn to Silurian Park.

"Robbie!" Madelyn VanEpp called out sharply, and then to Livvie, "Where on earth is that boy going?"

"To get the canoe," Livvie said.

"Why, of all the — " Madelyn VanEpp started after her son, but Livvie pulled her back.

"Let him go, Mrs. VanEpp," she said. "He's going to work it out of his system."

Madelyn VanEpp turned to Livvie. "Make him see that I understand," she said, confusion in her voice. "He'll listen to you. Make him see that I tried."

"Yes, ma'am," Livvie said. "He'll come by the farm. I'll look after him." And she thought: *It is time. He will come to me tonight, and I will comfort him* . . .

28

But at bedtime, back at the farmhouse, there was no sign of Robbie. Livvie began to worry. She put on her nightgown and her heavy wool robe and kept watch at her bedroom window, her lamp turned low.

A brisk wind was coming out of the north. She thought of Robbie out on the lake, his precious lake, paddling with a fury. Maybe he had gone to the Up Holly, she thought. It was nice to think of him going to the Up Holly. Mama was right: things changed.

Downstairs, the big hall clock struck ten. Livvie got an old Indian blanket from the chest at the foot of her bed, then tiptoed down the hall to her parents' room.

"Ma?" she whispered into the darkened room.

There was the sound of heavy breathing, then someone stirred.

"Livvie?" a sleepy voice answered. "Are you still awake, dear?"

"Robbie's not back yet, Ma."

"Shhh. You'll wake your father."

"I'm goin' down and wait on the porch. All right, Ma?"

"He might've just canoed on home, Livvie."

"No, Ma. He'll come to me first. He always has."

"All right, dear. Do whatever you think's best. Be sure 'n bundle up."

Livvie left the lamp burning in the window, then went down to the front porch and curled up on the swing. Her body seemed to tingle all over. It was the anticipation, she thought. Her body was responding to the anticipation of it.

She tried to stay awake but kept dozing off. It seemed terribly late when she heard noises down on the landing, and then saw Robbie come up the hedgerow and cross the elm grove.

"Robbie!" she whispered.

"Livvie?" Robbie answered. He peered into the shadows.

"Up here, on the porch!"

Robbie came up on the porch and sat down on the swing. Livvie made room for him under the blanket.

"Your ma's upset," she said.

"I know."

"Talk to her, Robbie. She knows how you feel. She really does."

"All right," Robbie said. "I'll talk to her."

"Did you go to the Up Holly?"

"Yes."

"I knew you would."

"I nearly tore down the sign."

"But you didn't, did you?"

"No. I started to, but I didn't."

"Even if you had, we'd just nail it up again."

"Shoot," Robbie said. "What's the use?"

"You mustn't talk that way, Robbie. You've got to stick it out. We'll find a way."

"That's what I thought out on the lake, but things look different when you get back."

"Was it good out on the lake?"

"It's always good out on the lake. It's the comin' back that's hard."

"You don't mean me, do you?" Livvie whispered. "It's not hard coming back to me?"

"No, Livvie. It's good comin' back to you."

Livvie drew herself up close to Robbie and felt his hands.

"Brrr!" she said, rubbing his fingers. "They're cold."

"Yours are warm," Robbie said. "You're warm all over . . ."

"Oh, Robbie!"

The swing squeaked softly, and the wind rustled in the

trees. Livvie was astonished by the sensations that had come over her body. She had heard it affected you that way, your passions building till you couldn't stop even if you wanted to, which she didn't. She ran her fingers through Robbie's hair. It was time. It was really and truly time —

"Come on," she whispered. She took Robbie's hand and gathered up the blanket. "Ma might hear us."

The door to the hayloft was open. A rope with knots tied in it hung down to the ground. Robbie boosted Livvie up the rope, then swung himself up.

"Over here, Robbie," Livvie whispered from the shadows.

She tamped down a place in the hay and spread the Indian blanket over it. The orange-and-black pattern showed clearly in the moonlight. She slipped off her robe and fumbled with her nightgown.

"You'll have to help me, Robbie," she whispered. "It's knotted."

She tilted her head against Robbie's shoulder. Robbie reached around to undo the drawstring at the neck of the nightgown. The nightgown fell open.

"Oh, Robbie!" Livvie whispered, her lean body pressing shyly against his. "I'm so excited!"

Robbie ran his hands over Livvie's shoulders and down her back. Her skin felt soft and warm.

"Remember when we used to go up to Frog Creek," Livvie said, "and swim in the raw? It's different now, isn't it?"

180

"Oh, yes, Livvie," Robbie whispered, letting his lips brush her ears. "It's different now."

Robbie was overwhelmed with Livvie's presence, the smell of her, the feel of her, the rapid beating of her heart against his chest. It must be a very small heart, he thought.

Suddenly he felt Livvie give a start.

"Robbie! Someone's coming!"

They held their breath listening. The wind rattled the tin dipper that hung from the pump outside the kitchen. Below them there was a scuffing sound, then the muted tinkling of a cowbell.

"It's all right," Robbie said. "It's just the Guernseys."

But the moment was lost. Robbie felt a shiver run through Livvie, and then goosebumps on her arms.

"Oh, Robbie!" she whispered, tears in her voice. "I thought it wouldn't matter, but it does." She spoke falteringly, her shoulders shaking with little sobs. "We'd be cheating ourselves. A wedding wouldn't mean anything. It would all be a lie, and we'd be cheated — "

Robbie held her tightly until she was all cried out.

"It's all right, Livvie," he said, stroking her hair.

Livvie looked up at him. Her moist eyes glistened in the moonlight.

"You're not mad?" she said. "Ma says it's different with boys."

"No, Livvie, I'm not mad," Robbie said. "I'm kind of relieved."

181

"Really and truly?" Livvie said, and giggled.

"Uh-huh," Robbie said, the tenseness draining out of him. "The thinking of it is different from the doing."

"Come on," Livvie whispered, and pulled him down into the hay. "We'll hold each other and talk of Loon Lodge. If we keep thinking of Loon Lodge, Chicago won't make any difference."

They curled up under the blanket, the sweet smell of the hay all around them and, outside, the moon and the wind and the stars.

"Isn't it lovely," Livvie said, "to know where you're headin' and where you've been and that there's a point to everything?"

"But things keep gettin' so complicated, Livvie."

"There's no gettin' around it, Robbie. Ma says life's one complication after another."

"Shoot, what's so complicated 'bout wantin' your own farm?" Robbie said. "If people'd just let a guy alone."

"Oh, Robbie," Livvie said, "it's no good blamin' others. Everybody's doin' their best. You've got to believe that, Robbie. You've just got to."

It was warm under the blanket. They clung to each other till long into the night. It was better this way, Livvie thought. After all, holding, her mother had told her, was the best part of it.

29

Charlie Barrow was back at his old spot in front of Arbuckle's the next day, hawking his worms and waving at the cars, but somehow it wasn't the same. The farm ladies gave him funny looks, and hardly anybody waved back.

Robbie stopped by to see him after lunch. A smell of burning leaves came from Silurian Park. Overhead, a flock of migrating ducks veered in off the bay, skimming the steeple of Holy Childhood.

"Teals," Robbie said, scanning the sky. "Green ones."

"They're early th-th-this year," Charlie said.

"It'll be an early winter, probably," Robbie said. "Ducks sense things like that."

Charlie looked pale and wan.

"You seem down in the dumps, Charlie," Robbie said. "Aren't you glad to be out of jail?"

"It's the c-c-cars, Robbie," Charlie said. "Nobody's w-w-wavin' back."

"Shoot, Charlie," Robbie said, "folks've just got out of the habit. They'll start wavin' back. Just wait."

But deep down Robbie wondered. It was the jail, he supposed. Folks thought differently of you when you'd been in jail.

Arbuckle's porch was cluttered with merchandise and produce — stacks of galvanized pails, racks of pitchforks and scythes, baskets of squash and apples. Robbie helped Charlie arrange a place for his worms at the end of the porch.

"Is Shorty still lettin' you make deliveries, Charlie?" Robbie asked.

"Not y-y-yet," Charlie replied.

The Swede came up Main Street in his pickup. Mr. Rosenfelder followed close behind in his truck. The Swede tooted and waved, then turned down toward the telephone office. Mr. Rosenfelder, with a load of pumpkins, pulled up at Arbuckle's.

" 'Afternoon, Mr. Rosenfelder," Robbie said. "They look like fine pumpkins."

"Never mind the pumpkins, Robbie," the old farmer replied. He leaned back against the truck. "Heard you was mixed up in the Herr Doktor business, is that right?"

"Yes, sir," Robbie said. "And Jim 'n Livvie too."

184

"Folks're upset, Robbie. A boy ought not interfere in grown-up affairs."

"Why not?" Robbie said. "Sister Joan Therese says justice is everybody's business."

Herman Rosenfelder shifted the wad of tobacco that bulged in his cheek. "Nuns!" he spat. "The Herr Doktor's closin' the tannery tomorrow. What's your highfalutin nun goin' to do about that?"

Robbie turned to Charlie. "Don't listen to that old crab, Charlie," he whispered. "C'mon, let's split a licorice."

A few farm ladies were milling around the counter when Robbie and Charlie came in. They looked up but said nothing. The bell jangled, and Mr. Rosenfelder came into the store. Robbie and Charlie waited at the candy counter. Herman Rosenfelder walked over and whispered something to Shorty Arbuckle. Robbie sensed a hostility in the air.

"Well, if that ain't the last straw!" he heard Shorty say.

Shorty weighed up a little pile of boiled ham on the scale, then came over to where Robbie and Charlie were standing.

"Beat it, Charlie," he said, motioning to the door. "I don't want you hangin' round here no more."

Charlie's mouth fell open. "B-b-but . . ." he started to say.

"No back talk," Shorty said. He shoved Charlie toward the door. "Just get your worms and scram."

Charlie went outside.

"What's the big idea, Shorty?" Robbie protested. "Charlie hasn't done anything!"

"I ain't goin' to argue, Robbie," Shorty said. "Now was there somethin' you wanted?"

The spell hit Charlie as he walked out on the porch. He stiffened up and fell into the stack of galvanized pails. The pile collapsed in a loud clatter.

Robbie ran out on the porch. Charlie was thrashing about violently, his legs flailing within an inch of the curved blades of the scythes.

Mr. Rosenfelder came out behind Robbie.

"Quick!" Robbie hollered. He dropped to his knees and clamped his arms around Charlie's chest to drag him away from the scythes. "Get a stick for his tongue!"

Herman Rosenfelder leaned back against the storefront and spat. "Troublemaker!" he muttered.

"What's all the racket out here?"

It was Shorty Arbuckle coming out on the porch. The three farm ladies were a step behind him.

"It's the defective," Mr. Rosenfelder said. "Ain't that an eyesore for the town? Oughta be in Mendota with his own kind."

"Lookit him!" one of the farm ladies sneered. "A regular ravin' maniac, and on account of him the tannery's shuttin' down!"

Robbie looked up in bewilderment. It was as if a great hatred had come over them, just like the seizure that had gripped Charlie, and there would be no helping it till it had run its course.

186

"Will somebody please help?" Robbie cried, struggling to keep Charlie from rolling off the porch. "I can't hold him by myself!"

Herman Rosenfelder laughed. "I'll help, Robbie." He drew back a foot. "A swift kick in the tail'll snap him out of it — "

Robbie lunged for Herman Rosenfelder's manure-caked clod as it came down on Charlie, and twisted hard. The old farmer toppled back against the storefront, pitchforks and apples clattering down upon him.

"Why, you danged scalawag!" he cursed, and started to get up. "I'll — "

But Robbie was already on his feet and had grabbed one of the pitchforks. Herman Rosenfelder fell back to the floor. Robbie waved the pitchfork menacingly under his nose.

"You leave Charlie alone!" he screamed, tears coming to his eyes. "You hear me? You just leave Charlie alone!"

Herman Rosenfelder stared up at Robbie, ashen-faced.

"You dasn't hurt me, Robbie," he gasped. "You dasn't."

Robbie felt his heart pounding and his muscles quivering. Something terrible was coiled up in him ready to snap, and he knew that once it snapped he would go wild with the pitchfork and wouldn't be able to stop —

"Robbie!"

Robbie felt an arm spinning him around. It was the Swede.

"Are you out of your head?"

Robbie looked up at the Swede and then down at Charlie. Charlie was coming out of the spell now, white-faced and weak, his voice barely a whisper.

"R-r-robbie —"

Robbie threw down the pitchfork. He and the Swede helped Charlie to his feet. The crowd on Arbuckle's porch watched in silence.

"C'mon, Charlie," Robbie said, gently. "We'll go down to the bay and watch the herons."

Charlie put one arm around Robbie and the other around the Swede. They started down the steps, Charlie's knees wobbly and his face streaked with sweat.

A car with Michigan plates turned up Main Street. Charlie started to wave at it, but he didn't have it in him.

30

The tannery was closed down all the next day, but reopened the following morning, the whistle blowing an hour earlier than usual to spread the word. Tom Armitage was there to greet the workers, and there were rumors that the Herr Doktor had spent two hours in Stanfill P. Stanfill's office, and that afterward Judge Koontz had been hurriedly called in.

The Swede had gone up to Hayward to deliver some cheese to the county hospital. It was late afternoon when he got back. Robbie was waiting out by the smokehouse.

"Well, Stan got more'n he was expectin'," the Swede said. "The Herr Doktor backed off on the will and pleaded guilty to a charge of conspiracy to commit arson."

"What'd he get?" Robbie asked.

"A year and a day," the Swede said. "Suspended."

"Shoot," Robbie said, "it don't seem like much, does it?"

"No, it don't, Robbie," the Swede said. "But Stan's very philosophical about these things. He figures the Herr Doktor'll get his, one way or another."

They went inside. Robbie brought in some logs and started a fire in the fireplace. The Swede got a pail of beer from the icebox and slumped into the big leather armchair next to the window.

"I saw Herman Rosenfelder up at the courthouse," he said. "He said he's glad the way things turned out."

"I'll bet!" Robbie smirked. "Shoot, I feel like goin' down and punchin' that dumb old crab in the nose."

The Swede seemed in a funny mood.

"Oh-hh, Herman ain't such a bad sort, Robbie," he said. "I'll admit it was pretty nasty what he did to Charlie down at Arbuckle's, but folks get nervous when a town's livelihood's at stake. Herman's probably kickin' himself for the way he acted."

"Bull!" Robbie said. "Shoot, folks around here'd sell their grandmother if there was a dollar in it, Stanfill P. Stanfill included."

The Swede leaped to his feet and yanked Robbie from his chair.

"You've got no call to talk that way about Mr. Stanfill, Robbie!" He shook Robbie hard. "It's men like Stan Stanfill that make the world go round. I've a mind to beat

190

the bejesus out of you, runnin' folks down and moonin'
'cause your daddy took a job in Chicago. Where's your
gumption anyway? Your daddy's doin' what he feels he
has to do, and it's up to you to help him —''

"I'm sorry, Swede," Robbie said. "It's just that —''

"It's just that you've been feelin' so sorry for yourself
you can't think straight."

The Swede let loose of Robbie and sat back down.

"You shouldn't be so hard on folks, Robbie," he said.
"Everyone's tryin' to get through life as best he knows
how, searchin' for a little joy and a friendly face and all
the while wonderin' when his number'll come up. Life
ain't easy, Robbie. 'Tain't easy at all . . .''

They sat there in silence for a while. The fire crackled
brightly. Across the lake lights were coming on at
Moonrise. Robbie got up to leave.

"Should I light a lamp, Swede?" he said.

"No-oo, Robbie. I think I'll just sit here."

"What's got into you, Swede, anyway?"

"Oh, I get awful blue this time of year, Robbie."

"Is autumn like this in Sweden?"

"Yah, 'cept the hills are steeper and it gets dark earlier.
We used to climb in the rocks along the fiord and watch
the boats come in out of the haze. Autumn was always
special. I was only five years old when we left, but I can
still picture it."

"Autumn's the best season of all," Robbie said. "It
wouldn't be worthwhile without autumn."

"But it gets me blue, Robbie," the Swede said. "I get

191

to wonderin' about things, and I get blue. And the more I wonder, the more futile it all seems, all the books and the philosophers and their highfalutin notions. And maybe that's the way it was meant to be, for us to keep searchin' and searchin' and never find the answer . . ."

He took a drink of beer and slouched deeper in his chair.

"But at night when I'm not quite asleep but not quite awake either it all comes back to me, all the sweet yesterdays, and I can smell the old smells and taste the old tastes and hear the old sounds. And I start wonderin' where it's all gone, and I get sad. Oh, Jesus, I get sad, and I wish someone was there to ease the sadness. So-oo — " he stretched his arms and yawned, "Millie 'n me are gettin' married, and then I'm joinin' the marines."

"The marines?" Robbie said.

"This country's been good to me, Robbie," the Swede said. "I figure if I join up now I'll be ready when the shootin' starts."

"But what if you get killed, Swede?"

The Swede stared out the window. The glow from the fireplace deepened the lines in his face and gave a hollow cast to his eyes.

"Nothin' comes free, Robbie," he said, softly. "Sooner or later we all have to pay the piper."

The Swede walked down to the pier with Robbie.

"Are we still friends, Swede?" Robbie said.

The Swede put a hand on Robbie's shoulder and squeezed it.

192

" 'Course we're still friends, Robbie," he said. "I was there the night ol' Doc Davies spanked your bottom. We'll always be friends."

Robbie climbed into the canoe and got ready to shove off.

"It's heck movin' away, though," he said. "I don't care what you say, Swede."

"We-ll, Robbie," the Swede said, "life's full of tricks. Sometimes you've got to go away so that you can come back again."

Later that night, alone in his room in the house on Arcadian Avenue, with the kerosene lamp turned low and a cold wind coming in the window, Robbie could hear singing coming from town hall. It was the quartet from Hugo's rehearsing for the harvest festival.

" 'Tis the gift to be simple, 'tis the gift to be free,
'Tis the gift to come down where we ought to be,
And when we find ourselves in the place just right,
'Twill be in the valley of love and delight."

Was he about to pay the piper? Robbie wondered. Was that what moving away meant, paying the piper for seventeen years in the valley of love and delight?

"Come on down, Son!" It was Madelyn VanEpp calling from downstairs. "I fixed us a snack."

There were doughnuts and cider waiting in the kitchen.

"It isn't easy, Son, is it?" Madelyn VanEpp said as she watched Robbie eat. "All the trouble, and now our moving away."

"No, Mom," Robbie said, "it isn't easy."

"But it wouldn't be any good to stay on in Sister Bay knowing we'd cheated your father out of his big chance, would it?"

"No, Mom, that wouldn't be any good either."

Madelyn VanEpp glanced around the kitchen, at the glass-doored cupboards and the cookstove and the red-checked oilcloth on the table.

"I'll miss this creaky old house," she said. "It's the only home I've ever known."

It had never occurred to Robbie that moving away might be just as difficult for his mother as it was for him.

"Well," he said, "at least we'll still have the kitchen table to sit around."

"Probably not, Son. Your father says the kitchen's too small for this table. He's put a down payment on a new one, with chrome legs."

"Mom?"

"Yes, Robbie?"

"I guess we're not hard up anymore, are we?"

Madelyn VanEpp sighed.

"No, Son," she said, "we're not hard up."

Robbie finished his cider and brought an armload of kindling in from the porch. The crisp smells of autumn came in the door.

"I'll miss October most," he said. "October's the best month of all."

"Yes, Son," Madelyn VanEpp said. "You're right."

Madelyn VanEpp looked in on Robbie after he was in

bed, a lamp in her hand and a spare comforter over her arm. Robbie's thoughts went back to when he was a little boy and his mother had held a lamp over him at bedtime to inspect him for wood ticks and bloodsuckers. It seemed so terribly long ago.

"You'll need extra covers tonight, Son," Madelyn Van-Epp said, pulling the comforter up tight around him. "That's a cold wind out there."

It made it easier, Robbie thought as he fell asleep, his mother's knowing that October was the best month of all.

31

Charlie set himself up at a new place to wave at the cars, in front of the Dew Drop Inn, but it wasn't as good as Arbuckle's, and only people in out-of-town cars waved back. Two days later he had another spell and was ordered to stay in bed indefinitely. Worry began to show on Violet's face. Charlie's spells had never come that close before.

The Barrows lived in a little white cottage above Silurian Park. Climbing roses twined through the picket fence and grew up the sides of the cottage. Charlie had planted the climbers when he was a boy.

Robbie dropped by the Barrows' after mass the following Sunday. Charlie looked tired and peaked. Violet said the spell had taken a lot out of him, and that his lungs were badly congested.

Robbie had brought along the plans that Livvie had begun drawing up for Loon Lodge.

"Will there be a place where I can w-w-wave at the cars?" Charlie asked.

Robbie studied Charlie for a moment.

"Is it that important to you, Charlie," he said, "wavin' at the cars?"

"It's how I f-f-fit in, Robbie."

"I don't understand, Charlie."

"It makes people feel g-g-good, Robbie," Charlie said. "They see you out there w-w-wavin', and they laugh and w-w-wave back, and pretty soon they fit you in."

Charlie's window looked down over the rooftops of the town. It was a bright day with a brisk wind that played tricks with the weather vanes. Robbie and Charlie sat there for the rest of the morning, talking about Loon Lodge and watching formations of ducks come down over the lake — mallards and canvasbacks and teals.

Later on, Charlie's mother, looking very tired, her eyes red and watery, brought in a tray of cocoa and pecan rolls. The rolls were warm and chewy, and there were little marshmallows in the cocoa. Charlie took a sip of the cocoa and began coughing. Mrs. Barrow burst into tears.

"Look at him!" she cried. "Nothin' but skin and bone! They've killed my Charlie!"

She looked very pathetic, Robbie thought, in her faded kimono and with tears streaming down her rouged cheeks.

Violet came in and motioned for Robbie to sit down.

"Come on, Mama," she said, taking her mother by the arm.

"We're goin' to Belgium next week, Robbie," Mrs. Barrow said. "Aren't we, Violet?"

"Yes, Mama."

They went out into the hall.

"When w-w-will you be leavin', Robbie?" Charlie asked.

"Oh, in a couple of weeks or so, Charlie."

"There's not much t-t-time, is there?"

"No, Charlie," Robbie said, suddenly feeling very weary. "There isn't much time."

When it was time to leave, Robbie gave Charlie their special handshake. Then he collected his missal and rosary and started for the door.

"Robbie?" Charlie said.

"Yeah, Charlie?"

"Even if we never b-b-build Loon Lodge," Charlie said, "it's been sw-sw-swell dreamin' about it."

Robbie had known Charlie Barrow all his life. He was like Cracker Jack and old shoes. But he had never felt as close to him as he did that lovely autumn morning with the weather vanes spinning and the mallards quacking and the taste of the marshmallows from the cocoa soft on his tongue.

"Shoot, Charlie," Robbie grinned. "A guy's got to have a dream."

Charlie rapped on the window and waved as Robbie

unlatched the gate on the little picket fence. Robbie looked up and waved back. Through the window, Charlie looked pale and thin in his flannel pajamas, safety-pinned at the neck, and with an afghan wrapped around him.

And as Robbie turned and walked up the street, he was filled with a dreadful certainty that the cycle of trouble had not yet ended.

32

On Tuesday, Charlie went into a spell and never came out of it. Violet said it was a blessing.

They laid out the body in the Barrows' parlor, but hardly anybody came by, and only a handful of people came to the cemetery. Robbie was so angry, tears came to his eyes.

"What's a guy to believe in, anyway?" he said to the Swede. "I'd believe in nothing, 'cept I don't know how."

"They're ashamed, Robbie," the Swede said. "They're ashamed over what they did to Charlie."

They buried Charlie on a little rise above the Ivors' plot. Robbie and Jim served as pallbearers, and as they lowered the casket into the grave, the sky cloudy and a damp wind coming up off the bay, it seemed to Robbie that all his childhood dreams were being buried with it. He thought of the time he and Jim and Charlie had found a dead heron washed up along the Low Holly. They had got a spade from behind Hauger's and given the heron a little funeral. Instead of saying prayers they had cawed. The cawing had been Charlie's idea. It seemed a better funeral than the one he got.

"May the choir of angels receive you," Father Baumgarten chanted, sprinkling the grave with holy water.

At that moment Mrs. Barrow collapsed in Violet's arms and let out a mournful wail that echoed out over the bay. Robbie thought of the Herr Doktor and tried to hate him, but the hate wouldn't come out, only a kind of stunned sadness. For he knew now that the Herr Doktor wasn't really to blame, just as he knew that Charlie hadn't died of his illness. Charlie started dying the day people stopped waving back. It didn't seem like much to do for a guy, Robbie thought, just to wave.

"Where do you think Charlie is now, Swede?" Livvie said as they walked from the cemetery.

"Oh, Charlie's still with us, Livvie," the Swede said, "in you 'n me, Jim 'n Robbie, all of us."

"Then nothing ever really dies, does it?" Livvie said. "Everybody is a part of everybody else, and it goes on forever."

"You might say that, Livvie," the Swede said. "Yah, that's a fine way of lookin' at it."

Later that day, as he had done so often in times of stress, Robbie walked over to Holy Childhood to see Sister Joan Therese.

It was dusk. A lovely autumn haze hung on the quiet evening air. Leaves crackled pleasantly underfoot. A light was burning in Sister's little office in the schoolhouse. Robbie tapped on the window. Sister Joan Therese motioned for him to come in.

"I've been expecting you," she said. "I figured you'd be out wandering around, trying to get your bearings."

"Yeah," Robbie said, forcing a little smile. "I figured you probably figured."

There was a little couch along one wall of the office. Sister came around her desk, and they sat together on the couch.

"So much dying!" she sighed. "But — it seems you aren't the only one who's got some adjusting to do. I learned today this will be my last year at Holy Childhood."

Robbie looked up, surprised. "Really?"

"Yes," Sister said, "they're finally putting me out to pasture."

"At the motherhouse?"

"Yes. Oh, it won't be the end of the world. I'll supervise the library and work on my science book. It's not far from Chicago. You must come see me. There is a visitors' lounge and a garden with a grotto."

"Golly," Robbie said, "the school won't be the same without you."

"Oh, I'll miss Sister Bay," Sister Joan Therese said. "There is goodness here, and respect. But — times are changing, people are changing."

The sound of organ music and singing came from the church where the adult choir was rehearsing.

"Bend Thou what is stiff of will,
Warm Thou what with cold is chill —"

"Has being a nun been hard for you, Sister?" Robbie asked.

"Oh, at times, Robbie," Sister replied. "But there can be no dedication without sacrifice. It is a kind of moral law, I suspect."

"I didn't mean that way, Sister," Robbie said. "I meant not having a family of your own and all."

"But I've never been without a family, Robbie," Sister smiled. "You and Jim and Livvie and hundreds like you, each one different, each one special —"

She looked up at the crucifix that hung from the wall behind the desk. In the shadowy light Robbie thought he detected a moistness in her eyes.

"And the parents — sharing their joys and their sorrows. Such richness! And now it's all winding down, like a tired old clock . . ."

They sat without speaking, listening to the singing in the church, and for a while it seemed to Robbie that none of the trouble had happened. Charlie would be up at Arbuckle's in the morning waving at the cars, and Wilma

Houtekier would have some chrysanthemum shoots for him to plant, and then on Friday he would canoe over to Moonrise and Alvia would read poetry in the summerhouse —

"You and Jim looked very handsome and grownup at the cemetery today, Robbie," Sister said. "I know Charlie is very proud of you."

"Is?" Robbie said, tightly. "Shoot, Charlie's dead and gone, and that's that."

"You don't believe that, Robbie."

"What else is there to believe?"

Sister Joan Therese took Robbie's hand and held it tight.

"You see it all crashing down on you, don't you?" she said. "I know, I know. But you mustn't let it destroy your faith, Robbie. You mustn't!"

"Shoot," Robbie said, "what's the point?"

"Listen to me, Robbie! There is a grand design, a great interdependence of things. Migrating ducks are able to navigate by the most distant star, and it is the same with people. Each of us serves an important purpose in God's work. You've got to believe that, Robbie. You've got to believe in the grand design, or else something inside you will wither and die."

"Oh, yeah? Well, what was the purpose in Charlie's bein' picked on and put in jail and kicked into his grave?"

"It's not for us to know, Robbie," Sister said. "Maybe the heartbreak of others is meant to help just a few of us to know, and through our knowing to keep the

204

world moving onward and upward to some wonderful state of grace that is beyond our comprehension.''

"Shoot, everything eatin' everything else, and people connivin' and cheatin' and killin'. What kind of grand design is that, anyway?''

And then in a deep wracking sob all the grief and hurt and disappointment that had been building in Robbie finally broke loose, and he burst into tears.

"Oh, it hurts!'' he cried. "It hurts so bad!''

He buried his head in Sister Joan Therese's lap, and for long moments there was only his muffled sobbing and Sister's soft, insistent whispering.

"Believe, Robbie! . . . Believe!''

33

And then came the bittersweet time, the time for chopping firewood and laying in hay, for mending snow fences and putting up fruit, as if the golden summer had been a mere prelude to the real business of the Northland, which was winter.

School began — it had been postponed while the children helped with the harvest against the threat of an early frost — but Robbie was excused from classes. There would be little point in his settling into the routine at Holy Childhood, Sister Joan Therese decided, only to be uprooted in a couple of weeks. Besides, she added, coming from a parochial school, he would be at least a year ahead of his class at the public school he would be attending in Chicago. Nevertheless, she loaded him up with an armful of books.

"An idle mind is the devil's workshop," she said.

Robbie missed school but welcomed the extra time to himself. One day Jim came down from the reservation on the creamery truck and stayed overnight at Robbie's. The two of them stayed up late, talking.

"I don't understand what you're poutin' about, Robbie," Jim said. "If the marines accept him, the Swede's goin' to put me in charge of things while he's gone. And Livvie'll still be here, won't she? And we'll have all the stuff from Moonrise, won't we? Shoot, I figure we'll be in good shape."

"But it'll be nearly four years, Jim," Robbie argued. "What if somebody buys that land before we come of age?"

And he vented the resentments that had been building up in him. It was all jobs, he had concluded. Shorty Arbuckle and Herman Rosenfelder, all of them, maybe all of history, even, Miles Standish and the philosophers and Hannibal crossing the Alps — all one mad scramble to see who got the jobs. There were two sets of rules, it seemed, one for what people said and another for what they did, as if everybody had secretly agreed, *"You believe my lies and I'll believe yours."* They whooped it up for Horatio Alger and the Golden Rule so long as it didn't threaten their jobs. But once you threatened their jobs, they would chew you up and spit you out and make you wish you'd never been born. Poor Charlie had made the worst blunder of all, Robbie said. He had called their bluff. Simply by being Charlie, by being weak and sick and vulnerable and easy to take advantage of, he had called their bluff. And they had turned on him and tried to ship him off to Mendota to keep their jobs safe. It was a crock of bull. All of it. It made you want to puke.

Livvie Buhl worried about Robbie's hardening attitude.

"It's as if he's all bitter inside," she told Sister Joan Therese. "He says it's a crummy town, and that we ought to pull up stakes before we end up just like everybody else."

"Give him time, Livvie," Sister Joan Therese said. "He sees his world collapsing around him. Pray for a glimmer of grace."

And so every morning before school Livvie would slip into church and light a candle.

"We've so little time," she prayed to the Blessed Virgin, "and I'm scared that if he leaves feeling this way he'll never come back."

Slowly, a healing process seemed to take place. Indian summer had come. The days were pleasantly warm and hazy, and the nights cold and clear. Everybody said it was the best autumn in fifteen years. Robbie fell into the habit of meeting Livvie every afternoon when classes let out, and there were long, lovely walks home from school, the streets filled ankle-deep with fallen leaves and the houses decorated with colorful arrangements of corn shocks and gourds.

208

"It's hard to stay mad when it's autumn," Robbie said one day and broke into his familiar grin.

They stopped by the Dew Drop Inn that afternoon. Violet treated them to chocolate malteds made with the new electric mixer. There was enough to fill a tall glass twice and little packets of vanilla wafers that made a crinkling noise when you opened them. Robbie noticed Violet was wearing pumps instead of her old tennis shoes, and that she looked somehow different.

"Millie Horton fixed my hair." She primped and smiled anxiously. "Do you like it?"

"Oh-hh, it's lovely, Violet!" Livvie said.

Her mother hadn't had a drop since Charlie's funeral, Violet said. It was a miracle. And Horace Ward from the Red Crown station had taken to dropping by. They had gone to the show up in Hayward last week and were going again on Sunday.

Livvie giggled with delight. "Vi-o-let's got a sweet-heart!" she chanted in a singsong. "Vi-o-let's got a sweet-heart!"

One morning, shortly after breakfast, Robbie was surprised when two of the farm ladies who had been up at Arbuckle's the day Charlie had the spell came by the house. He sneaked up the back stairway while the ladies visited with his mother in the parlor. They gossiped about the Sodality and the new tannery contract and offered to help when the moving-van came. When they left, they gave Madelyn VanEpp a box of homemade fudge with marshmallows and pecans for Robbie to eat on the train.

"I feel like mixin' it with manure," Robbie said when he told Livvie about it, "and tossin' it up on their porches."

"Robbie!" Livvie exclaimed in dismay. "They're tryin' to make up. Can't you see? They're sorry for what they did, and they're tryin' to make up."

As the days slipped by, Robbie and Livvie seemed to develop a new awareness of each other. Livvie was ecstatic.

"It's my season, Ma," she said to her mother, "the most wonderful season of all."

"Oh, there'll be others just as wonderful, Livvie," Lela Buhl sighed. "Life has a way of makin' you ready for things when they happen."

There was a sort of quiet languor to their new relationship that both Robbie and Livvie found pleasing. They held hands and laughed a lot over nothing and touched each other frequently, but there was none of the urgency of that night in the loft. Robbie was glad. There was a proper order to things, he was discovering, and urgency could ruin it.

At night, out on the swing, there would be shy little probings, sweet and unhurried. "It's almost a spiritual thing, isn't it?" Livvie whispered. "Getting used to each other's bodies."

The town watched the unfolding romance with great interest.

"Livvie Buhl's finally blossomed!" the farm ladies said up at Arbuckle's. "And ain't it a joy to behold!"

210

But there were skeptics.

"You just watch, he'll get down there with them high-steppin' city girls," scoffed Shorty Arbuckle, "and that'll be the end of Livvie Buhl. Mark my words!"

But even Shorty admitted they made a nice couple, and whenever Robbie came into the store he was especially attentive to him.

Robbie was aware of all the talk but paid it no heed. Deep down, however, there was a gnawing fear that he and Livvie were living on borrowed time. He had seen families move away from Sister Bay before. They left reluctantly, tearfully, but when they came back to visit it was different. They put on airs and poked fun at the outhouses.

"Don't worry, Robbie," Livvie said one night out on the swing. "If you want a thing bad enough, it'll come to pass."

She covered his face with feathery little kisses, like a rabbit — his lips, his cheeks, his eyes. Her lips felt cool and sweet and moist, like a willow grove after a rain.

"Are you sure you want it bad enough, Robbie?" she whispered.

"Yes, Livvie, I'm sure."

Livvie pulled the Indian blanket up around them and took Robbie's hand.

"Then don't worry, silly," she whispered. "It'll come to pass. Oh, your hand's so warm! Yes, there . . . and there . . . oh, Robbie!"

The days dwindled. Preparations for the harvest festival

neared completion. Robbie spent all of one day helping with the decorations, and when he had finished and Main Street was festooned with bright orange bunting, he was filled with a great sense of loss. He would leave, and the life of the community would go on without him. There would be no hunting the Flambeau with Jim, no Thanksgiving with the hills snow-covered and the houses filled with good smells, no Christmas with the tree in Silurian Park all lit up and the carolers singing and the farmers coming to town in their horse-drawn sleighs, bells jingling and the breath of the horses pluming up in the crisp winter air.

"It works both ways, Robbie," Stanfill P. Stanfill said when Robbie ran into him up at the post office one morning. "The town will miss you too."

"Shoot," Robbie scoffed, "how d'you figure that?"

"A boy fills the community with his youth, Robbie. Folks see him out there canoeing up the lake or tramping through the woods, and they feel better for it. Then when he's gone, there's an emptiness."

Soon it was time for Robbie to start making the rounds saying his goodbyes. Everybody had a nice word and joshed him about city life.

"Reckon you'll be a regular slicker next time we see you, Robbie," the farmers joked up at the post office. "Yessir, all brilliantine and bay rum, maybe spats, even." And they all had a good laugh.

Madelyn VanEpp gave Robbie a loaf of banana-nut

212

bread to take along when he went over to see Mr. Houtekier. Odie had a little going-away present for him. "Wilma snipped it before she — passed on, Robbie." It was a clematis shoot rooting in a little glass jar. "She said be sure and mulch the roots in the winter."

Odie Houtekier looked gaunt and tired. Since his wife's death he had kept to himself. He sat out on the porch in the evenings, and at night a candle always burned in the room where Wilma had died.

"Will you be stayin' on in Sister Bay, Mr. Houtekier?" Robbie asked.

"No-oo, Robbie," Odie replied, "I think not. I haven't been able to adjust, you see. Wilma and I were together a long time, and I can't adjust. Life's short, Robbie. I noticed you've been cozyin' up with the Buhl girl. Grab hold, boy. Grab hold while you can . . ."

Livvie went along with Robbie when he canoed up to Moonrise to see Mrs. Armitage. They found her out by the stables, raking leaves. She smiled and waved, and it was as if all the trouble had never happened.

"I've been expectin' you, Robbie," she said. "You'll have time for a bite, won't you?"

The grass had been cut, Robbie noticed, and the stable door repaired, and everything looked clean and bright. But he was amazed to see children running about everywhere, a dozen of them at least.

"Holy cow!" he cried. "Where'd they all come from?"

There were two families living at Moonrise now, Mrs. Armitage explained, her nephew Tom's and her niece Loretta's. The house was so big and the rooms had been empty for so long.

"Moonrise is finally the happy house Arthur Ivors had hoped it would be," she said.

On the way back they stopped off at the Rosenfelder's farm. Robbie had wanted to avoid it, but Livvie insisted.

"You've got to leave with a clean slate, Robbie," she said.

Mr. Rosenfelder showed them his new tractor and then took them up to his pumpkin patch.

"Pity you won't be here for the harvest festival, Robbie," he said. "Your pumpkins look mighty good this year."

"Shoot, your pumpkins'll win," Robbie said. "They always do."

"We-ll, they don't win by accident, Robbie." Mr. Rosenfelder dug into his overalls and pulled out a little envelope. "Here, I've been savin' these for you."

Robbie opened the envelope. "Pumpkin seeds?" he said.

"They're special, Robbie. Took me years to develop them. If you ever get your place on the Up Holly, plant just a few hills at first and keep the best ones for seed."

The old farmer walked back down to the canoe with them.

"One thing's been botherin' me, Robbie," he said.

214

"The other day up at Arbuckle's — you wouldn't have used that pitchfork, would you?"

Robbie looked Mr. Rosenfelder square in the eye. "Yes, sir," he replied, "I would have."

At first Herman Rosenfelder seemed taken aback, then he shook his head and chuckled.

"Figured as much," he said. "And I'll tell you somethin' else. Best way to make a friend is to have a brawl with him."

He shook Robbie's hand and mussed up his hair.

"Well, Robbie, the tractor's yours to borrow whenever you start bustin' ground on the Up Holly."

When they got back to town, Millie Horton came running down to meet them.

"It's the Herr Doktor!" she said, out of breath. "He's had a stroke, in his compartment on the *South Wind* goin' down to Florida. They say he can't cope no more. They're bringin' him home tonight on the local — "

That night, a little crowd gathered at the depot. They took the Herr Doktor off the train through the baggage car, on a stretcher. And so all the old adages were true, Robbie thought. Waste not, want not. Grasp all, lose all. He thought of that day up in the courthouse and felt very sad. The Herr Doktor had done cruel things, but then nobody had invited him over. Maybe it all would have been different if folks had invited him over.

"But who'll look after him?" Livvie whispered.

And then a woman climbed down from the baggage car

215

behind the stretcher and began issuing orders in a firm manner. She was middle-aged and somewhat stout, but with friendly eyes and a nice smile.

"Saints alive!" Lela Buhl gasped. "Gerta Brandt's come back! Well, maybe now he'll have a chance to set it all straight."

34

On Robbie's last day, he and his mother packed his bags into the car and drove up to Buhl Farm, where Lela Buhl was having a going-away dinner for him.

Jim had come down from the reservation, the Swede was there with Millie Horton, and even Shorty Arbuckle dropped by to pay his respects.

He had been down to Eau Claire the day before, Shorty said. There were lines in front of the recruiting stations, and he'd heard that several local boys had run off and joined the Canadian air corps.

"Insanity, that's what it is," Lela Buhl said. "Youngsters runnin' off to war with the fuzz still on their cheeks."

"Every generation has its war, Lela," Shorty said. "There's no gettin' around it."

The Swede, in his Sunday best, had already taken his physical for the marines.

"Healthy as a horse," he grinned, thumping his belly with a fist.

He would be sworn in to the reserves, he said, and then return to Sister Bay to await a call to active duty, probably in spring.

"I look for us to be in it by summer," he said. "The French'll turn tail. You watch!"

Shorty Arbuckle said the United States would probably go to war against Japan too.

"The Japanese?" Livvie said with surprise. "But they make such lovely toys."

There was a funny mood toward the war, Robbie had noticed. Everybody said it was a shame, but seemed anxious for the United States to get into it.

Millie Horton talked excitedly about her wedding plans. Violet would be maid of honor, she said, and there would be a big reception at Andy's Tavern.

Lela Buhl got very sentimental. "Oh, I'm so happy for you, dear!" she said to Millie. "It'll be nice havin' you for a neighbor, won't it, Henry?"

The Swede said Millie had been fixing up the shed to have it ready for Jim. There would be curtains and a bunk bed and a stove, and when electricity came in, maybe a radio.

"Pity you won't be here, Robbie," he said. "I was

218

figurin' on you to be best man. Guess I'll just have to make do with ol' Menabozho here.''

Robbie slapped Jim on the back.

"Hey, Jim!'' he grinned. "That's swell!''

They had dinner by candlelight even though it wasn't dark yet. There was baked ham with parsleyed potaoes and acorn squash from the garden. Lela Buhl had fixed her special peas, creamed in a thick cheese sauce and mixed with tiny onions, and there were platters of fried eggplant and tomatoes and hot baking-powder biscuits with jam and honey.

"Hard times are like a hot spell,'' the Swede said, his mouth stuffed with food. "When they're over it's like they never happened.''

The Swede had brought over a pail of Old Style Lager. Lela Buhl and Madelyn VanEpp got very giddy. They danced around the kitchen singing "Oh, Them Golden Slippers'' and then collapsed in each other's arms, their cheeks flushed and their eyes bright and shiny.

"Oh, it's been a joy havin' you close by all these years, Madelyn!'' Lela Buhl sighed, out of breath. "Where has it all gone?''

She looked at Robbie and Livvie holding hands under the table.

"Seems only yesterday they were fishin' the Narrows for the first time,'' she said, her eyes misting up. "They're born, they grow up, they're gone. You try to protect them, to hang on to them, but finally you've got to let go, and all you can do is keep the hearth warm so's they'll have a place to come back to if they stumble and fall. Oh, the sweet sadness!''

Everybody laughed and joked and had a fine time. It was nice, Robbie thought, the way they all pulled together to make his going away easier.

"Now you be sure 'n wear your galoshes when it snows, Robbie," Livvie said. "It gets terrible sloppy in Chicago."

Jim laughed. "Shoot, Livvie," he said, "how d'you know? You've never been to Chicago."

"Well, I've seen the newsreels, haven't I?" Livvie said. "Chicago gets sloppy in the winter, and folks line up for blocks to get bread."

The Swede had hysterics.

"Breadlines are a thing of the past, Livvie," he said. "Even in Chicago."

For dessert there was Livvie's applesauce cake with nuts and raisins and a dollop of whipped cream. Afterward, Robbie and Jim and Livvie walked down to the landing and skimmed rocks off the lake.

The sun was going down. The air was cool and misty. The lake was quiet and still and shimmered in the twilight. Sounds carried out over the water, clear as a bell — dishes clattering, people laughing, screen doors slamming. Up at Andy's the juke box was playing.

> "There'll be love and laughter
> And peace ever after,
> Tomorrow, when the world is free —"

As they were starting back up to the house, Livvie burst into tears.

"Oh, it doesn't seem possible!" she sobbed. "It's been barely a month, and yet our whole world has fallen apart. We'll never put it back together again, never in a million years."

She buried her face in Robbie's shoulder.

"Don't worry, Livvie," Robbie said, stroking her long chestnut hair. "I'll figure something out. Maybe I'll just run away."

"Shoot, you can't do that, Robbie," Jim said. "A guy's got to stick with his family."

"But I'm old enough to join the navy now, Jim," Robbie said. "I could send my pay to you 'n Livvie for Loon Lodge."

"Oh, Robbie, you can't do that!" Livvie said. She dried her eyes and took his hand. "It would break your ma's heart. You're all she's got, and it would just break her heart. And your pa's too. He loves you, Robbie. He may not show it sometimes, but he does. You can't buy happiness with someone else's sorrow — "

And then it was time to leave for the depot. Livvie and Jim and the Swede ran down the pasture alongside the car, waving and hollering their goodbyes — Livvie in her red-checked gingham jumper and the Swede in his Sunday best and Jim with the cardinal feather sticking from his hat, and behind them the blue lake, smooth as glass, and the green hills and the orange-and-purple sky. A V-shaped flight of geese was coming in over the Up Holly, heading south.

221

"Take it slow, Robbie!" Jim hollered as the car went out of sight. "Take it slow!"

Then they turned and started back up the pasture, Livvie in tears and clinging tightly to the Swede.

Henry Buhl watched the scene in the pasture from the kitchen window. It pained him to see his daughter so distressed. Ernest would have been Robbie's age if he had lived, he thought, and Howard two years older. National Guard age.

He turned hurriedly to his wife.

"Lela, tell Livvie to fetch a sweater and meet me round at the truck. And ask the Swede if he'd mind runnin' Jim up to the reservation."

"Lands, Henry!" Lela Buhl exclaimed. "Where're you off to in such a dither?"

Henry Buhl swung open the screen door and started out toward the barn.

"Those kids've got somethin' precious, Lela," he called back. "And it strikes me that if we're goin' to help them we'd best do it while there's still time."

222

35

It was nearly dark when Robbie and his mother pulled up at the depot. A hint of frost was in the air. In the distance, a train whistle echoed plaintively.

Robbie was surprised to see Sister Joan Therese and Violet and Mrs. Barrow waiting to see him off. There was a flurry of excitement.

"We're sayin' a novena for you and Loon Lodge, Robbie," Violet said, "and Mama knit you some mittens."

Sister Joan Therese presented Robbie with a book, Willa Cather's *O Pioneers!*, and lectured him on his responsibilities.

"There's a lot of notions loose in the public schools, Robbie," she admonished. "Be critical, be selective!"

Madelyn VanEpp straightened her son's tie and pinned his ticket and baggage stubs to the inside of his jacket.

"Give your father all the help you can, Son," she said. "No whining or complaining, understand?"

Robbie looked up the tracks. The headlight of the *Limited* was coming into view. The sky behind it was dark blue and the stars were coming out. He had never thought there would be a time when he would hate to see the *Limited* rounding the bend.

"Enter my pumpkins in the harvest festival, will you, Mom?" he said. "And try to display them next to Mr. Rosenfelder's."

The train ground to a stop in a shower of soot and cinders. As Robbie started to gather up his things, his mother broke into tears.

"You're a good boy, Son." She hugged Robbie close to her. "I'm proud of you."

Mr. Reitmeyer, the conductor, waved to them as he swung down to the platform.

" 'Evenin', Madelyn," he said, tipping his hat. " 'Evenin', Robbie. Heard you folks was plannin' to move."

"Yes, Tom," Madelyn VanEpp said. "We're finally making the break."

Mr. Reitmeyer took out his gold railroad watch and eyed it as they talked.

"Folks're comin' and goin' all up and down the line, Madelyn," he said. "Makes a body wonder where it's all takin' us, the TVA and hydramatic drive." He turned to

224

Robbie. "Won't seem the same without you hangin'
round the depot, Robbie."

"Oh, I'll be back," Robbie said.

"Sure you will, Robbie," Mr. Reitmeyer said, quietly.
"Sure you will." He looked at his watch. "Well, you'd
best hop aboard."

Robbie kissed his mother, then handed his things to the
colored porter, a rotund man with a shiny face and a wide
smile.

"Don't you worry none, ma'am," the porter smiled.
"We'll look after the young man."

There was the clanging of bells and the rumble of the
locomotive and the waving of lanterns. Robbie clambered
aboard.

"God bless you, Robbie!"

"Stick to it, Robbie!"

"Goodbye! . . . Goodbye! . . . Goodbye! . . ."

Robbie made his way back to the observation car. The
train was crowded. The porters were making up the
berths. There was a smell of cigar smoke and fresh lin-
ens. A few pairs of shoes had been set out to be shined
during the night.

"Boar-rd!"

There was a lurch, and the train started moving. Robbie hurried out onto the observation platform and leaned
over the railing to wave to his mother. But Madelyn Van-
Epp was walking up toward the parking lot, her back
turned to her son. There seemed to be some sort of commotion. The train rumbled slowly down the tracks. Rob-

bie felt hurt. You always waved until the train was out of sight; it was good manners.

Then he spotted Henry Buhl's old pickup skidding to a stop in the parking lot. Livvie jumped out and raced down the platform.

"Robbie!" she cried. "Oh, Robbie!"

"Livvie! What's wrong?"

"It's going to be all right!" Livvie called up to him, laughing and crying at the same time. "Pa's going to sign the homestead papers!"

Livvie caught up to the train. Robbie reached down and grabbed her hand.

"But I don't understand — "

"Pa telephoned your father in Chicago. He said if you'll at least give college a try it'll be all right for you to come up summers and live with us. Pa'll pay you fifty cents a week to help with the chores and the rest of the time we can work on Loon Lodge — "

The train was almost at the end of the platform.

"It's second-best, Robbie, but maybe if we work hard we can make it first-best — "

Then the platform ran out. Livvie pulled back her hand and stood there waving, slender and lovely in the soft evening light.

"Stick to it, Robbie!" she called after the train. *"Stick to it!"*

And then she was gone.

The train curved into the woods and began to pick up speed. It would follow a steep grade around Thunder

226

Ridge, then wind down out of the hills and race southward through autumn-tinged valleys and along silver-hazed rivers, its whistle echoing reassuringly across the sleeping countryside.

Robbie stared down at the tracks. The sensation of riding backwards made it seem as if the train was going where it had just been. Full circle, Sister Joan Therese had said. Life was a process of coming full circle. And the Swede — you've got to go away so that you can come back again. All the sweet people. It was as if the town were a great repository of wisdom. But there must be other towns just like it, all over the country, all over the world, little repositories of wisdom —

"Good evening, son."

Robbie looked up. A portly man in a double-breasted suit had come out on the platform.

"Good evening, sir," Robbie replied.

"Catching a bit of air?"

"Yes, sir."

The man took out a long black cigar and motioned back down the tracks.

"That town we just passed through," he said, "what was the name of it?"

"Sister Bay, sir," Robbie said. "Sister Bay, Wisconsin."

The man leaned back against the railing and lit the cigar. The rich tobacco smell mixed pleasantly with the cold night air.

"Seemed like a nice little town," he said.

The train rounded a hill, and Big Chetac came into view below them, long and smooth and silvery in the moonlight. The lights of Sister Bay flickered in the bluffs.

"Yes, sir," Robbie said. "It's a fine town."